Keeping Secrets

Keeping Secrets

By
LeAnne Hardy

Birch Island Books
St. Paul, MN

Acknowledgements

This book has been many years in the making and passed through the hands of too many readers to mention. Some were South African, some American; some experts in the field of HIV and AIDS, some skaters, and some lay readers just looking for a good story.

Any understanding I have of life in Tembisa comes from the children of Arebaokeng and Bophelong Empilweni after-school programs and the faithful workers who support them.

Thank you to Russell Merton for answering questions about the legal procedure Uncle Njabulo would bring, and to Dolly Gouden for scanning sample legal documents. If you are a South African lawyer and those scenes don't sound real to you, it's my fault, not theirs.

Thank you to the skaters at Kempton Park who let me be part of their community for the three years I lived there. Thank you to Peter and Trevor who have pushed me on the ice, and to Brian who taught me to call "toe picks" "toe rakes."

I could not have produced a polished manuscript without the hard questions of my critique group, Wynee, Celia, Mark, Sara, Stephanie, Pat, Lorenz, and Mary.

Special thanks to Rachel Fredland, Mseleni, KZN, who has seen up close the impact of HIV, and to her friends and family members who corrected cultural misrepresentations. Thanks also to Susan Binion, Susan MacDonald and Bonnie Zama for their points of view.

Thanks to Erika Hazelton for her careful proofreading. Any mistakes that remain are purely my own.

A huge thank you to my husband who believes in me so much that he moved back to Africa when I wanted to write for children affected by HIV and AIDS. What would the past forty years have been without you?

Lastly, thank you to God, the Source of joy in the face of suffering, for adopting me into his family and for allowing me to participate in what he is doing in the world.

Glossary for American Readers

Sindi is South African. The terms she uses are natural expressions for her. I have tried to make the meanings clear enough in the context for non-South African readers, but just in case you are confused, here are some translations.

baba	father
bakkie	pickup truck
bin	See dustbin
boerewors	local sausage
bunk school	cut class, play hooky
catapult	slingshot
Christmas crackers	tissue paper tubes with prizes inside that guests pull apart at Christmas dinner
cool drink	soda pop
crèche	daycare
dustbin	trash can or wastebasket
eGoli	Zulu name for Johannesburg, place of gold
exercise book	notebook
Gauteng	The province that is primarily the metropolitan areas around Johannesburg and Pretoria
gogo	grandmother or old woman in isiZulu
inyoni	bird
isiXhosa	language of the Xhosa people
isiZulu	language of the Zulu people
izangoma	plural of sangoma, traditional healer
Johannesburg	largest city of South Africa, founded on gold mines
Jozi	a popular nickname for Johannesburg
kombi	van
kraal	corral
KwaZulu	place of the Zulu people, part of the modern province of KwaZulu-Natal or KZN
late	passed away, dead
learners	students

lorry	truck
matric	final year of secondary school
mealies	dried corn
molo	isiXhosa greeting
molweni	plural form of isiXhosa greeting
Mpumulanga	The province between Gauteng and KZN
nappies	diapers
nursing sister	nurse (not a nun)
packet	bag
palisade	fence of vertical metal rods
pap	very firm cornmeal porridge
Pretoria	The executive capital of South Africa, about half an hour north of Tembisa
rand	South African currency
revise	review
robot	traffic light
sangoma	traditional healer
sawubona	isiZulu greeting
school head	principal
shebeen	unlicensed bar
sikhokho	You burn the pot, Zulu slang for good job
sisi	sister
stationary supplies	school supplies
sweets	candies
tackies	sneakers
taxi rank	like a bus station for shared taxis
toe rake	toe pick (the points on the front of a skate blade)
tsotsi	gangster
umlungo	derisive word for white person
umakhulu	isiXhosa for grandmother
washing powder	detergent
Woolies	Woolworths, a classy department store
yebo	yes, I agree

Prologue

I remember what it was like Before. I flew over the ice like a swallow on the wind. Music filled my whole body, and I soared like a bird above the city of Johannesburg—eGoli—place of gold. I dreamed of gold medals and going to the Olympics someday.

But that was Before.

I was too young to know that life can collapse as fast as a skater can lose an edge and tumble to the ice. It hurts to fall, but you get up; you keep skating. You smile for the judges, and you don't let them see the pain. That's what winners do.

But sometimes, the hurt is too much, and you can't get up. You can't keep skating.

Then you lose.

Chapter 1

The pounding pulse in my ears threatened to drown the announcer's voice on the loudspeaker. "Please welcome our next skater, representing the Skating Federation of South Africa—Sindiswa Khumalo!"

"You'll do great, Sindi," my American coach, Trevor MacDonald, murmured beside me. "Just relax and have fun."

Relax? Not likely with all those people watching. If they knew the truth, would they still cheer? I shook the tight, beaded braids that covered my head and tried to absorb the calm in Mac's eyes. Breathe, Sindi. Breathe. Don't think about home. Forget your parents. Focus.

I pushed away from the gate. My arms spread wide to receive the cascading applause as I skated a broad arc toward center ice. Mac's voice sounded in my mind. *Smile for the judges.* Even he didn't know my secret. I stretched my lips into an expression intended to sparkle.

I searched the stands for my parents although I knew they weren't there. The friends I had made in a month of training camp cheered enthusiastically from the back rows. Someone whistled and stomped as if this was an American ice hockey game.

Ben. It had to be Ben.

The audience grew quiet as I took my starting pose—spine arched, head back, one arm raised like a graceful branch toward the high curve of rafters. I swallowed hard, but the smile never slipped from my face.

The music started—the theme from *Out of Africa*. I let it pull me across the ice, flowing in deep edges and vaulting in tight jumps. My spiral sequence went straight into a double-Axel/toe-loop combination jump. The double loop halfway through the program nearly tripped me up, but I bent my knee deep and held onto the landing. I didn't expect to win—not in my first American competition. After all, this was Lake Placid, where some of the best skaters in the world trained. But I did hope to skate clean. My final combination spin went from position to position, perfect balance, perfect centering, thanks to Mac's relentless coaching and hours of practice.

I had never skated better in my life.

The music stopped. I froze in my final position, eyes closed to hold back tears. If only my parents were here to see me!

I took my bow, smiling and waving while stuffed animals rained on the ice. I swept up a monkey and a fat hippo on my way to the gate. Little girls in matching blue skating dresses came on to clean up the rest.

Mac hugged me as my father would have. "Perfect! I am so proud of you, Sindi." That was what my father would have said: I am so proud of you. Only he would have called me "Nyoni"—bird—for the way I flew over the ice.

"Get your skate guards on." Mac took the stuffed animals from my hand. "There's someone I want you to meet."

I held his arm for balance while I wiped the slush from my blades and slid the plastic guards over them. A little girl in blue thrust a large plastic bag toward me.

I frowned at it. "What's this?"

"Your presents." She gestured at the ice.

"All these?"

She giggled, and another little girl held out a second bag.

"You're popular." Mac handed me my blue warm-up jacket with the Lake Placid logo embroidered on the front. Tomorrow I would go home to South Africa, but I would keep the jacket forever.

"Leave your gifts in the locker room and come on." He led me out of the arena and down a corridor, pausing for me at the locker room door.

"What about the scores?" I trotted after him as quickly as my blades in their clunky plastic guards allowed. The next skater's music already played behind us.

"They'll be posted in the lobby. Don't worry. It'll take a few minutes. We have plenty of time." Mac stopped in front of a room marked "VIP Hospitality" and ushered me in. A buffet table at one end was covered with salads and fruit. The smell of crisp, hot rolls tickled my nose.

"There you are!" A woman set down her glass of white wine and stood. She was as tall as Mac, and the skintight clothes on her long thin body made her seem even taller. Her hair was short and curly and very blond. Diamond earrings sparkled when she shook her head. She came toward me with her hand held out. "You were marvelous, Sindi. Absolutely marvelous!"

I shook her hand politely and glanced at Mac for a clue.

"Sindi, I'd like you to meet Amanda Etherington," he said. "Amanda, this is Sindi." He was grinning like this was a special occasion.

"Oh," I said, suddenly understanding. "The lady who loaned me the dress." I glanced down at the pink lace and chiffon studded with hundreds of Austrian crystals that my parents never could have afforded. "Thank you very much for letting me use it. I'll take it off as soon as they have posted the results. But I think …" I glanced at Mac. "I think Mac wanted to have it cleaned first."

Ms. Etherington waved a long elegant hand. "Forget the dress, darling. It's yours. It's perfect on you."

I stared at her openmouthed before I could muster the presence of mind to say thank you for the amazing gift. A designer dress like this cost hundreds of dollars.

She led me to a chair beside hers. "Now sit down. I want to talk with you." Everything about the way she moved and dressed said that she was young, but something about her face didn't fit. A hint of sag? Tightness where there ought to be wrinkles? Under that blond hair color, I was pretty sure there was gray.

Ms. Etherington looked at me. "Mac says you have had a very good summer."

"Well, I was only here a month, but I learned a lot. Mac is a wonderful teacher."

"I know. He trains all my skaters. How would you like to stay here and train with him?"

"Stay here? In Lake Placid?" The beads in my hair rattled when I shook my head. "I would love to, but the Federation only sent me for a month. My family can't afford—"

"Yes, yes, I know. But what if I were to pay your expenses? You could stay in the dorm again or live with a local family. I spoke to Jenni Cameron's father about the possibility. I believe you girls are friends, aren't you?"

"Yes, ma'am." My stomach fluttered with excitement so I could hardly get the words out. Stay in Lake Placid? Train with the best? Jenni Cameron had introduced me to girls who had been coming to Lake Placid summer skating school for years. That had made all the difference between being an exotic stranger from Africa and having friends.

"You could go to school with Jenni. They make special arrangements for the skaters so you'll have plenty of time to practice. I would pay for your coaching, your costumes, your entrance fees."

"It's called a sponsorship," Mac put in, seeing my confusion. His eyes urged me to say yes.

I looked from him to Ms. Etherington and back, uncertain. "But what would I do in return?"

She laughed, a deep, guttural laugh. "You would work harder than you have ever worked in your fifteen years or I will send you straight back to South Africa."

"I'm a hard worker!" I said.

"That's what Mac has told me, and I was certainly impressed with the results today. I suggest that we try the arrangement this season." She looked at Mac as if for agreement. He nodded. "And then we can re-evaluate."

So I would be on trial. Coming here for the Federation was pressure enough, but this? What if she found out about my father? Would she still want me?

"I don't understand. Why would you want to pay my expenses?" My parents had pulled themselves out of poverty before there was any such thing as affirmative action in South Africa. They would not want me to accept charity even though there was nothing I wanted in the world more than to skate and to train here with Mac.

Well, one thing.

Ms. Etherington leaned back in her chair. "Because I love skating, and a competition is always more fun when I have invested in one of the skaters. I think an investment in you could take me a long way. Maybe even to the Olympics."

The Olympics? I had had dreams, dreams I never even told my parents, dreams that seemed far beyond possibility from my home rink in a shopping mall outside Jozi—Johannesburg. My heart pounded in my chest. This was my chance, my chance to go for the top.

"I'll need to talk to my parents."

"Of course you will." She picked up her glass of wine and sipped. "And you'll need to change your flight. Mac can make all the arrangements." She was obviously not used to hearing no.

A timid knock sounded at the door. It opened and Jenni Cameron stuck her head in. "Excuse me." A mischievous grin lit her face when she glanced at me. "Sindi won. They're waiting on her for the awards ceremony and pictures."

"I won?" My mouth fell open.

Ms. Etherington smiled. "Didn't I say you would be worth the investment?"

* * *

Jenni was on the podium next to me—second place. She bubbled over with happiness in her green- and gold-sequined dress. We were only intermediate skaters, but medaling at Lake Placid was still a big deal—a very big deal. Jenni's father stood on the sidelines with Ben Bradley and a bunch of our other friends. I think Ben had a crush on Jenni. He whistled when our names were called.

When the official pictures were done, I handed Ben my phone. "Take a picture for me, please." I pulled Jenni close. We held out the medals around our necks and grinned for the camera. *Click.*

"Thanks."

"We're gonna miss you, Sindi." Ben slung his arm over my shoulder in that friendly American fashion that I was starting to like. "Will you be back next summer?" Ben would be competing on the Junior Grand Prix circuit this year. He was on a fast track to the top, and to think that Ms. Etherington was offering me a chance to go there too!

I glanced at Jenni and wondered if anyone had said anything to her yet about the possibility of my staying with them. "Maybe," I told Ben.

He handed me the phone, and I touched the numbers to send the picture to my older sister, Jabulile. Jenni and Ben wandered off with her father while I sat on a bench and took off my skates. I left them under the bench and pushed my mother's number as I walked into the sunshine outside. The phone rang and rang. I clicked off before it could switch to voice mail. International calls were too expensive for leaving messages. I pushed Jabu's number instead. Surely she would answer.

"Sindi? Sindi, is that you?"

"Yes. It's me." I waited for her to say something about the picture. Surely she could see that the medal was gold. She wouldn't need me to tell her I had won.

"Thank God you called. Baba's worse. A lot worse. Mama took him to the doctor today for some tests. I don't know what the doctor said, but Mama's upset. She's shut them both in the bedroom and won't come out. So it might be me or Solly at the airport to pick you up instead of Mama."

"But you can't drive."

"So? I'll take a taxi. If we're not there, you just wait. You'll be all right, won't you?"

"Of course I'll be all right." I may have been only fifteen, but I traveled halfway around the world by myself to live in a dorm in a strange town with other skaters and train with a new coach. I could wait in the Johannesburg airport for a few minutes until someone came for me.

Jenni Cameron crossed the parking lot, arm in arm with her father, dragging her wheeled skating bag behind her.

"Jabu," I began. I wanted to tell her about the sponsorship, but she spoke at the same moment.

"I'm so glad you're coming home tomorrow. Baba wants to see you badly. He needs you. I'm so afraid ..." Her voice faded.

I put my finger in my other ear to block the sounds of traffic on the Lake Placid street. "What was that, Jabu?"

"Never mind," she replied. "We'll see you when you get here. We'll be together as a family, and that's all that matters."

I sat on the bench a long time after hanging up. I hadn't said anything about staying in Lake Placid. I hadn't told Jabu about Mac or Ms. Etherington or the sponsorship. The sun was hot through my brown tights. I was beginning to sweat in the beautiful dress made for the cold of the arena, not the warmth of a summer afternoon.

I got up slowly and went back inside for my skates. I smiled weakly and waved at the friends who greeted me in the lobby. The dressing room was empty when I got there, scattered with tights and skates and smelling of makeup and hairspray. I stripped off the elegant dress, hung it back in its nylon garment bag, ready to return to Ms. Etherington, and slowly packed my belongings.

Mac met me outside the locker room. "Did you talk to your parents?"

I shook my head. "I can't stay, Mac. My father's very ill. I have to go home. My family needs me."

"What's wrong with your father? I didn't realize he was sick."

No one gave my father's illness a name. No one said out loud what I was sure of in my heart. "They did some tests today. Maybe they'll know more in a few days." They knew already. Why else would Mama shut herself in the bedroom? But I couldn't tell Mac.

"Oh, Sindi. I'm so sorry."

From the look in his eyes, I was sure he was thinking it was something like cancer. He slid an arm around my shoulder and gave me a hug. Tears stung my eyes, and I felt guilty for letting him think that. I wished it *were* cancer. You can talk about cancer.

Chapter 2

My older brother Solly came with Jabu to meet me. They were there when I came out of the bright new Johannesburg customs hall and waved the gray plush hippo I was carrying. They might have been arguing, but they stopped when they saw me.

Jabu waved and smiled, showing her white teeth. "Welcome home!" she cried in an unnaturally cheerful voice. A few strangers leaning on the barrier, waiting for other travelers to arrive, smiled. My big sister's mass of tight braids brushed my cheek as she gave me a hug. "I'm so glad you got here," she whispered.

Solly took my suitcase. "How was America? Love the hippo!" He slapped it affectionately.

"I saw the Statue of Liberty from the airplane," I said as we crossed the wide marble arrivals hall. The smell of hamburgers and KFC drifted down from the fast-food places on the open mezzanine above us. "Mostly I was inside an ice rink just like here."

Solly laughed and wiggled his eyebrows.

"Oh, Solly, I wish you could have seen me." Solly had started on the ice with me when we both were small—before he switched to inline skates. "Did Jabu show you the picture?"

"What picture?"

"Forgot." Jabu shrugged, motioning us through the glass doors.

"Jabu! That was a gold medal around my neck!" When would I ever have a chance to win another important one like Lake Placid?

"Gold medal? *Sikhokho*! You burn the pot!" Solly stopped long enough to give me a high five. He was less than a year older than me. Jabu was a year older than Solly. I think my father's traditional Zulu family was pretty pleased when we showed up one right after the other but after me, my modern, urban mother said enough was enough.

The late afternoon light was golden, and the air outside was cold. American summer had disappeared in the long, transatlantic flight, and this was Southern Hemisphere winter at seventeen hundred meters—almost six thousand feet, my American friends would say. I shivered and tried to think where I had packed that Lake Placid warm-up jacket.

"Come on!" Jabu led the way across the wide access road toward the crowded parking garage.

We passed the towering InterContinental Hotel and reached the out-of-the-way pavilion where the buses and kombi-taxis picked up people who couldn't afford the hotel shuttles and metered taxis by the main doors.

We climbed into a white van with the bright colors of the South African flag painted down the side. My family owned a car. I hadn't ridden in shared taxis very often. In America Jenni already had her learners permit, but the age to drive in South Africa was eighteen. Jabu was still seventeen.

I sat next to a large woman in a cleaner's uniform smelling of disinfectant. She had a handbag big enough to hold my ice skates, my warm-ups and a half dozen costumes.

The taxi soon filled with airport employees whose shifts were ending, and the driver nosed through the maze of access roads. He looped around onto the R21 expressway, filled with rush-hour traffic, and exited a few minutes later into the familiar streets of Kempton Park. I had lived in Kempton Park all my life.

Until a couple months ago, that is.

When the kombi pulled into the taxi rank between the railroad tracks and a row of bustling shops, I looked longingly up Pretoria Road toward our old neighborhood of Glen Marais. There sat the house I grew up in with its landscaped gardens and swimming pool. All the houses in Glen Marais had swimming pools. Not in Tembisa.

I didn't say anything as I followed Jabu and Solly across the gravel lot to change for a taxi to the former African township where we now lived. At least Jabu and Solly had figured out taxis. I said nothing as we rode. Crowded taxis weren't the place to talk about personal business, and I felt tired and disoriented from long hours in an airplane.

The streets of Kempton Park slid by. I turned my head to see the mall with the ice rink and Solly's skate park. The golf course across the road looked lush and green from winter rains.

"We need to save some money," my parents had explained when we moved. "For your skating," my father added, although he had never complained about the cost of my skating before. But then he became ill so often he had to take early retirement from the Finance Ministry. The doctor bills mounted.

A wide expressway whisked the taxi north through an industrial area. An "informal settlement" spread out to the left now instead of the golf course. That was what they taught us to call them in school—the areas where shacks made of scrap lumber or sheets of roofing sprang up overnight with no zoning or public services like water or sewers. There was usually electricity. Clever people knew how to splice wires onto the main lines and avoid paying the power company.

We left the informal settlement behind and pulled up to the stoplight by the new shopping mall. The vendors in the makeshift market in the vacant lot across the street were packing up their stalls and going home for the evening. Jabu made us get out at the corner near the police station. Solly dragged my suitcase behind him, weaving between the masses of faces, so much darker than most of those in Lake Placid. The suitcase bumped over the rough ground where the sidewalk ended, past the green palisade of Tembisa Library. It was all very—African— a different world from where I had spent the past month. A different world from Kempton Park.

We turned right at the church. The unpainted cement-block building squatted in the middle of a bare-earth yard. It didn't have a steeple like our church in Kempton Park. Or colored glass in the windows. It just had a sign: WONDERFUL WORDS OF LIFE CHURCH. Then in smaller letters underneath: JESUS SAID, "I HAVE COME THAT YOU MIGHT HAVE LIFE AND HAVE IT MORE ABUNDANTLY."

I looked at the children lined up outside a shed near the back of the lot where another sign hung over a garden gate: FIGHT AIDS WITH GOOD NUTRITION. The toasty smell of rice and chicken came from the shed. Children left the front of the line with plastic plates of food and sat on the church steps or under a straggly tree to scoop it up with their fingers in the traditional way. Was this what they meant by abundant life?

Further down the block, Jabu stopped in front of the solid metal gate Mama had insisted on installing before we moved here. Our house in Glen Marais had a wall. All houses in Africa had walls. Most of them these days had razor wire or broken glass on top. But in Glen Marais the gate was decorative wrought iron. Not here.

"I need my privacy," Mama had insisted. Leah Khumalo grew up in the township before apartheid ended and Nelson Mandela was elected president. You would think she would feel at home in Tembisa, but I think she was afraid.

Jabu fit the key into the lock of the pedestrian entrance. She hesitated. Her eyes slid sideways toward the cluster of people hanging out by the brightly painted metal shipping container on the corner where the public phones were. COMMUNITY CHAT was written on the side. I hadn't been in Tembisa very long before I went to America, but it had been long enough to be told that was where to go if I wanted drugs—which I didn't!

"Hey, Makatso!" Solly called and waved. I whirled around and stared at him.

"What?" Solly demanded.

I wasn't going to accuse him—not my own brother. I looked down the street to see who he was talking to.

A tall young man lounging against the container unwound his arm from the neck of a pretty girl and waved. The crowd of boys and young men around him looked our way. I recognized James from my class last term. Why was I not surprised to see James hanging out where the drugs were said to be?

"Hurry up, Jabu," I said. James was not someone I wanted to meet outside of class.

Jabu unlocked the gate, and we entered the tiny yard with its big jacaranda tree.

"Sindi!" Mama greeted me with an enthusiastic hug, but I didn't miss the look of relief that passed between Jabu and Solly. Mama was no longer locked in the bedroom with Baba.

The smells of curried beans, mealie pap, and my favorite tomato-and-onion relish filled the house. "I have made a feast for your return. Solly, take Sindi's suitcase to her room, and then we can eat."

This house was much smaller than our old one. I still felt like a stranger as I followed Solly into the bedroom I shared with Jabu. Our twin beds were pushed against opposite walls, but they came so close that if we sat on our beds facing each other, our knees would touch. My old skating posters were taped to the wall: Michelle Kwan, Kim Yu-Na, Ashley Wagner. But Jabu's fashion posters decorated her side of the room. My trophies lined the top of the bookcase. My medals hung on the post of my bed. I took the new one out of my bag and added it. I missed Jenni already.

Solly's inline skates stuck out the top of a cardboard box wedged between the wardrobe and the wall. There were only two bedrooms in this house, and Solly slept in the lounge.

"Sindi!" my mother called. "Come carry your father's dinner to him. He's eager to see you."

She smiled broadly as she held out a plate of food. A purple bruise darkened the inside of her silky brown arm. She had had blood drawn too. The same test as Baba? When she saw me staring, the smile faded. She pulled her arm back quickly and turned away. "Go on now. Baba's waiting."

My hands trembled as I carried the plate into the bedroom. It didn't have much on it—not as much as Baba used to eat—but there was a little pile of yellow pap and a spoon of relish beside it.

"Nyoni!" Baba's face glowed, although his skin, the color of ashes, hung loose on his bones. I tried to smile back, but it felt as if Sindiswa Khumalo were trapped inside, manipulating the muscles and peering out the eye-windows of someone else's body.

The room was crowded with boxes of things from our old house in Kempton Park—things we had no space for here. I moved a carved ebony lamp from the dresser to the heap beside the wardrobe and set down the plate, then turned to help the stranger in my father's bed.

Baba shivered under a pile of winter blankets and coughed slightly as he raised himself on one elbow and struggled to shift higher on the pillows. Fresh bandages covered the sores on his arms. Someone at the clinic must have cleaned them. Usually that was my job.

"You have come home, Nyoni." My father's eyes looked out from the thin face. "I am so glad."

The sound of singing could be heard from the church on the corner. I settled Baba on his pillows. "Here's your dinner. Now you be good and eat it all."

He smiled. "I'll try."

I sat on the edge of the bed while he took his first few bites. "You're going to get better, aren't you, Baba?"

He hesitated while he concentrated on swallowing his pap and relish. I wondered if his throat hurt him again. "Of course I will. The doctor gave me medicine." He patted my hand with fragile fingers, not the strong hand I used to hold to cross the street.

"I wish you could have seen my competition," I said. "I won."

He smiled, and I glimpsed the old Baba in his eyes. "I'm proud of you, Nyoni."

"Maybe I can skate the same program for the ice show in December." I still had the dress. Ms. Etherington had refused to take it back, insisting she had given it to me. "When your father gets better, then you'll come here to train," she had said as though it were a fact. "We have an agreement, you know."

I looked at my father now and wondered if he would ever be healthy enough for me to train halfway around the world. Or if Ms. Etherington would still want me if she learned the truth about his illness. "You'll be well enough to come to the ice show, won't you?"

This time he hesitated even longer. "I wouldn't miss it for anything," he said at last.

Chapter 3

Early Monday morning Jabu took me to the rink at Kempton Mall for the six a.m. ice time. "You don't need to mention that Baba is sick again, all right?"

"I'm not stupid," I said. "Aren't you coming in? Mama always sits on the bleachers with the other parents."

Jabu shook her head so the little beads on the ends of her braids rattled. Her eyes were rimmed with tightly curling black lashes, and it was easy to see why the boys liked her. "There's no way I am going to sit there and smile while Lerato's nosy mother peppers me with questions."

I left her sitting on a bench outside in the early morning light, examining her face in a little mirror and putting on more lipstick as though Mama always stayed in bed in the morning.

Inside the coolness of the empty mall, the sounds of my footsteps bounced back and forth between Woolworths, King Pies, and the little shop with the sparkly necklaces in the window. *Don't tell. Don't tell*, rang in my mind with every step. Of course, it would be okay to tell Lerato and Nicola. They'd been my best friends since signing up for skating classes when we were six.

A cleaning lady looked up from her mop and smiled. I held my head up and pretended I was at a skating competition. *Don't let the judges see how nervous you are.* That's what Mac said. I waved and smiled. The cleaning lady waved too.

"Look who's back!" Lerato called when I came through the glass door to the rink.

Nicola Brodowski ran to me, her blond ponytail bobbing behind her. "Sindi!" She threw her arms around me. "Was it fun? Were there any cute boys?"

I thought of Ben's mischievous grin. "Yeah. Some."

Nicola's mother, head coach Elaine Brodowski, didn't smile when she looked at me. "Are you ready to take your next test?"

I nodded. "I think so."

She laughed through her nose. She might be my friend Nicola's mother, but it wasn't a nice laugh. "We'll see."

The other skaters gathered around. Everyone except Mariki was looking at me. My regular coach, Liselle, patted my shoulder. "Did you have fun?"

"It was great. We skated for hours every day, and had ballet classes, and even a trampoline class to work on jumps."

Kobus's mouth fell open. He was ten and had curly yellow hair. All the girls liked him—even Mariki, who was older than Jabu.

Mariki tried to pretend she was too busy tying her skates to pay attention. She was pretty upset when the Federation sent me to Lake Placid even though she was older and had passed more tests. Mrs. Brodowski leaned against the boards and said something to her.

I looked back at Liselle. "I worked hard, and I learned a lot, and …" I took a deep breath. "I won the Intermediate Ladies Competition."

Lerato and Nicola squealed. Kobus cheered as loudly as Ben. Liselle gave me a hug. It was safe to tell them that much. I just couldn't mention Ms. Etherington. If I did, Liselle would say something to my mother, and my mother would send me back. But I couldn't go back. Not now. Not with Baba so sick, and Mama … Did she have a blood test? I didn't want to think about what it might have shown.

"Get your skates on," Liselle said. "I want to see what you've learned. And the rest of you get to work. It will be time to go to school before you know it."

Lerato's mother smiled a welcome as I pulled my skates from my bag. "Where's your mother this morning?" she asked. *Don't tell.* "I haven't seen her the whole time you were gone."

I sat down and began taking off my shoes so I wouldn't have to look at her. "She's at home. Jabu brought me."

"Your mother isn't sick again, is she?" MakaLerato did volunteer work at a clinic somewhere and always thought people needed to see a doctor.

"No," I lied quickly. "She's fine." I buried my face in my skate bag so she wouldn't read the secret in my eyes.

I warmed up during Kobus's lesson. The ice felt solid and normal beneath my blades, no different from the ice in Lake Placid. I had a good lesson. Liselle was pleased with all I had learned, and I flew like a bird, my heart full of music and movement and the laughter of my friends. When my lesson was done, I collapsed on the bench beside my bag, a grin of satisfaction on my face.

Nicola plopped beside me. "Guess what!" She pulled on my arm and whispered in my ear. "I saw Mariki at Mug and Bean with Johann van der Walt. They were holding hands."

"No!" I giggled. Johann won the men's Junior Nationals last year. He was a good skater and very good looking even if he did have pimples on his face and a piercing through his lip that looked like a sneer from a distance.

Nicola wiggled her eyebrows and grinned. She always seemed to know everything about everyone at the rink.

Lerato threw herself on the bench next to us. "Hi." She didn't even have time to catch her breath before Nicola was telling her about Mariki and Johann. Suddenly I knew I couldn't tell Nicola about my father being sick. It was a secret. Nicola wasn't good at secrets. A door as solid as the gate at our new house seemed to clang shut between us.

"Let's get something to drink." Lerato stood and pulled us after her to the kiosk. "Chips and hot chocolate," she said as she laid her money on the counter.

MakaMboti put the chips on the counter and ran hot, foamy chocolate from the machine at the back of the kiosk. African women were often called by the name of their firstborn. Not like the women I met in America.

I looked around for Mboti. He was way older than we were—maybe twenty—but he always said hi and cheered when I skated. I didn't see him in the pro shop where he usually worked or in the ticket booth. His mother handed the steaming cup to Lerato.

"Lerato!" Nicola whispered urgently and jerked Lerato's jumper so she almost spilled the chocolate. "What did I tell you?"

"What?" Lerato gave her a puzzled look. "Oh." She glanced at MakaMboti and backed away holding her cup without even saying thank you.

MakaMboti wiped her hands on her cotton skirt and looked at Nicola. Her face grew still as a store mannequin under her wool cap. "Don't forget your chips," she told Lerato in a flat voice. Lerato swiped them off the counter as though she were trying to get away with stealing.

MakaMboti turned to me. "And what would you like, Nyoni?" She used the same Zulu pet name as my father.

I shook my head. "Nothing, thank you." Snacks didn't cost much, but my family had too many other places to spend money these days.

"Yes, you do," Nicola insisted. "We want two hot chocolates." She turned to me. "I'll pay."

MakaMboti turned her back to fill the chocolate cups. Nicola wrapped her arm through mine and leaned her mouth close to my ear. "You must make her put the cup on the counter," she whispered, "and *then* you pick it up. You must never let her touch you."

"Why not?" I whispered back.

Nicola's breath was a warm, damp hiss in my ear. "Mboti is dying of AIDS. That's why he lost his job."

I stared at her. A vice seemed to close on my chest so I couldn't breathe.

Nicola pursed her lips and nodded slowly.

Don't tell! Don't tell! my mind screamed with every wild beat of my heart. Slowly I picked up my cup of chocolate from the counter and put it to my lips. It tasted like poison.

Chapter 4

As the taxi pulled into the traffic on Swart and headed toward Tembisa, I felt myself shrinking. Not because the taxi was crowded. It wasn't. Most people went *to* Kempton Park at this hour, not away from it. But the part of me that felt as big as the whole world when I danced over the ice retreated into a secret place deep inside when I went to school. Sindiswa the Skater became so tiny she could hide in the heel of my shoe. I didn't dare let her out, or the kids would think I was even more stuck up than they already did, just because I came from Kempton Park and used to go to school there.

I picked at the mustard-colored cotton of my uniform. It reminded me of the disadvantaged children we collected stationery supplies for last year at my old school.

The taxi stopped at the corner, and Jabu and I got out. A poster screamed from the wall opposite the taxi stop: KNOW YOUR STATUS; GET TESTED. I looked quickly away.

I should have defended MakaMboti to Nicola. You can't get HIV from hot-chocolate cups.

But I didn't.

Groups of uniformed learners milled around the courtyard of the high school. Maybe it was a good thing I didn't have any friends here. That way I wasn't tempted to tell anyone what was going on at home. Or what was going on inside of me.

"Are you all right?" Jabu asked.

"I'm fine."

She gave me a wary look as she went off to join her class.

Takalani stood just inside the gate. She tried to make it look as if she were waiting for someone, but I suspected she was trying to avoid the bully boys in our class—James and his friend Thabo. I couldn't blame her.

"Hi, Sindi!" Takalani called. "Were you sick?"

"No. I … I was visiting friends." I couldn't exactly say I had spent winter break in America. If word got around, kids would really think I was a snob. The bell started to ring, and we ran to class.

* * *

"Life Skills" our first class was called, whatever that was supposed to mean. Miss Diniso frowned when I handed her my pass. She didn't ask why I had missed the first week of the term. She only checked the paper work.

"Take your seat. You will have to copy someone's notes. You missed a lot of important material." Last term Miss Diniso used to smile when I read well or was the only one who could answer her questions. Today she sounded as cross as Mariki.

I slid into my seat and took out my lined exercise book. Takalani glanced at me from across the room and smiled. If I weren't so afraid of giving away the secret, we might be friends.

Miss Diniso began. "Last Friday we were talking about germs. Who remembers where we catch cold germs?"

Boring. I tore a blank page from the back of my exercise book and found a pen. Maybe Takalani would let me copy her notes.

"That's right," Miss Diniso said. "Cold germs are in the air and on things we touch."

The pen was dry. I sucked the tip for a moment and tried again. "Dear Takalani."

"Sindiswa?" Miss Diniso stood over me.

"Yes, miss?"

"I asked, 'What does HIV stand for?'"

I stared at her, and my heart stopped beating. How did she know?

"You weren't listening, were you?" She must have forgotten what a good student I was. She grabbed my paper, crumpled it, and threw it in the dustbin. I stared at the white buttons on her blouse and prayed that she wouldn't ask me any more questions about HIV.

"We are talking about the human immunodeficiency virus—HIV. Now pay attention."

"Yes, miss." I slid down in my seat and listened.

"Who can tell me the name of the disease caused by HIV?"

"AIDS," someone said.

James, sitting at the desk in front of me, kicked Thabo, and they both looked at Takalani. She wasn't smiling anymore. She stared at the floor as if she wished she were elsewhere as much as I did.

"Correct," Miss Diniso said in a loud voice that made my head hurt. She wrote the letters A-I-D-S on the board. "It stands for Acquired Immune Deficiency Syndrome." The chalk squeaked as she drew a line under each letter. "You cannot get HIV the same way you catch a cold. The human immuno-deficiency virus lives in the blood and other body fluids. It can't live in the air. It does not stay on things that a sick person touches like doorknobs the way cold germs do."

James and Thabo snickered, and I wanted to kick them to be quiet.

"You cannot get HIV from food prepared by an infected person, or by sharing dishes." Miss Diniso glanced at Takalani, but Takalani didn't look at her. Miss Diniso's lips were smiling, but her eyes were not, as if she were reciting something she had learned but did not believe. "Playing with someone, hugging them, even kissing them won't make you sick."

Thabo puckered his lips and made quiet kissing noises in Takalani's direction, but Miss Diniso didn't seem to hear.

I slid my eyes toward Takalani's back without turning my head. Did she have HIV?

"Now, what are the ways in which the virus is transmitted?" Miss Diniso asked.

An uncomfortable knot formed in the pit of my stomach while the class talked about drug addicts sharing needles, razor blades for traditional initiation rites and babies getting HIV in the birth canal or from mother's milk. My father was Zulu, and I was pretty sure he hadn't been initiated. I knew he didn't use drugs, but somehow …

"There are medicines that the mother can take before the baby is born that will keep her baby from getting the virus," Miss Diniso explained.

Takalani's face was still as stone. Did her mother have HIV? Is that how she got it? I forced my eyes back to my desk. I was being ridiculous. I didn't even know that Takalani had HIV. James and Thabo would bully anyone.

Miss Diniso continued. "It is very important, if you or anyone you know gets pregnant, that you should go to the clinic and have a blood test to see if you are HIV positive and need the medicine."

The boys snickered. Thabo pointed at a fat girl in the class. He stuffed a book under his shirt and patted it as if it were a baby.

See? I told myself. *He'll bully anyone. It doesn't mean a thing.*

Miss Diniso droned on. "There are other ways a person can get HIV." She explained about getting infected blood into a cut and why it was important not to touch anyone's blood. "Especially if you are caring for someone with HIV who has open sores on their body. You must always use plastic gloves when touching a sick person's body fluids. The virus can enter your body through only a small scratch or cut."

My heart fluttered in my chest as I examined my hands under the desk. There was a bloody hangnail on my right thumb and a small cut on a finger where I had wiped slush from my skate blade too quickly this morning. How many times had I had similar cuts when I washed Baba's sores? There were no gloves at our house.

"Can you tell by looking if someone has HIV?" Miss Diniso asked.

"No," the class answered in unison. We all knew that was the right answer, but Thabo poked Takalani in the back, and he and James snickered. I glared at them.

"How else can a person get HIV?" Miss Diniso went on.

Karabo finally said it. "Sex." He pushed his glasses up on his nose and didn't even look embarrassed. Thabo and James nearly fell off their chairs laughing.

Miss Diniso ignored them. "Yes, by engaging in sexual intimacy with an infected partner. Using a condom can reduce the risk of exposure to the virus. Not using a condom is called 'unprotected sex'. "

I was glad she hadn't called it "making love." My father loved my mother. He loved us. He didn't love whoever had given him this virus. I stared at the healing hangnail on my hand.

* * *

"Hi, Sindiswa." Pretty Mogane smiled and gestured me toward the cluster of popular girls in the shadow of the school building at break time.

What did she want? I was surprised she remembered my name. She usually called me "coconut"—brown on the outside and white on the inside. In the month I had been at this school before my trip to America, I must have told her a half dozen times that she couldn't copy my homework. She was older than me. At least as old as Jabu. Whether she had started school late or had to repeat, I didn't know. What I did know was that I was the youngest in my class—another thing that made me stand out.

But there stood Pretty, smiling sweetly, and beckoning me with her hand.

Impress the judges, I reminded myself as I put on a smile. *Just like a competition.* The circle of girls opened and closed around me. I was inside, surrounded by smiling faces.

But Pretty's smile had turned to something like the leer of a hyena who had found a weak or wounded animal. I hesitated. I might have backed away, but the cluster of girls stood close.

She cocked her head. "My grandmother saw you at the mall in Kempton Park."

My eyes darted from one expectant face to another. "Lots of people go to the mall."

She did a bad imitation of my city accent. "Lots of people go to the mall." The other girls laughed. "It was early in the morning. Before the shops open. My granny is one of the cleaners." Pretty casually examined her purple fingernails.

My pulse quickened. I licked my lips.

"She says you were there with a bunch of white girls. At the ice rink." The word "white" bit like sharp teeth. She arched her arms over her head in a mock ballerina position and circled on her toes to the laughter of the others. "Gran says you go every day. She says you're good."

It was not a compliment. She said it as if skating and working for an Olympic medal were something shameful.

For a brief moment Sindi Skater exploded out of the heel of my shoe where I had tucked her before school. My chin came up. I glared at this girl who had no goals that I knew of except to get the sugar daddy who paid her school fees to buy her jewelry and cosmetics.

"Coconut," someone whispered behind me.

I whirled around, but I couldn't be sure which girl had said it.

Someone laughed. "Do you have to paint the brown on in the morning? You know if you waited until after skating, maybe those *umlungos* wouldn't see the difference."

Sindi Skater shrank back into the heel of my shoe with a whoosh like a tissue caught in a vacuum cleaner.

"But they do," another girl said. "They always see the difference. No matter how good you are you'll never be one of them."

Sindi Skater was gone where they couldn't touch her, and I wished the ground would open and swallow plain Sindiswa Khumalo. I pushed my way out of the circle of girls. Their laughter cackled like chickens in the market. I wanted to run, but if I did, they would know how they had hurt me. I held my chin up and walked away with what I hoped was calm dignity. Their cruel comments nipped at my heels like naughty puppies. When I reached the end of the school building, I rounded the corner and leaned against the wall out of sight, breathing deeply and trying to slow the thumping in my chest.

I pulled out the bread and jam my mother had made for me last night. The blood test that bruised her arm must have revealed her status, but it was a secret even from her own family.

"You can't get HIV from food prepared by an infected person." That was what Miss Diniso had said. I opened my mouth and took a bite.

"You're going to die! You're going to die!" A crowd of

boys taunted Takalani at the far side of the schoolyard. Thabo poked her with a stick, and another boy threw a rock. Takalani raised her arm, but the stone hit her forehead over her eye and a trickle of blood ran down the side of her face.

"Leave me alone," she said.

Was that infected blood? I wondered. I looked around for a teacher to make the boys stop, but the teachers stood in a knot by the school, talking. They didn't see what was happening.

James shoved Takalani toward the gate of the compound. "Get out of here before you infect us all."

"You touched her!" Thabo laughed like a six-year-old. James wiped his hands on his clothes as if he was so stupid he thought HIV could be wiped off like jam from his fingers.

I leaned against the school building. The sandwich churned in my stomach. First MakaMboti, now Takalani. If I defended her, maybe they would think that I had HIV too. Or that someone in our house had HIV. If they knew …

The school head strode through the crowd. "What is the meaning of this?"

I pressed my back against the brick wall and pursed my lips to stop their trembling. I was glad I hadn't sent Takalani that note. Being friends was too dangerous.

The head's voice rose shrill and angry. "Wash that blood off your face and get inside the classroom immediately." But she didn't touch Takalani—not even Takalani's arm that didn't have blood on it. The school head was as scared of HIV as the boys.

When the bell rang, I went back to class, but Takalani's seat was empty.

Chapter 5

A dark man with a smile as broad as his middle stood outside our gate when we got home from school. He barely came up to Solly's shoulder, but then my brother was so tall most people thought he was a lot older than sixteen.

The man offered his hand. I shook it politely. So did Jabu and Solly.

"Good afternoon." His voice was deep and kind. "Is Everest Khumalo in? I am Pastor Oscar from Wonderful Words of Life." He gestured to the church on the corner.

My brain began to chant, *Don't tell! Don't tell!*

The pastor's brown suit was frayed around the cuffs, and his faded shirt didn't match his tie. "I understand he is ill," he said. "I thought he might appreciate a visit."

Solly glanced nervously at the little children peeking through the gate of the crèche across the street and at the loiterers outside the Community Chat. I think he was wondering who told on us.

"Our father was sick last week," Jabu said quickly, "but he's at work now. So is our mother. We aren't allowed to have anyone in."

Pastor Oscar nodded. If he knew she was lying, he wasn't going to accuse her. "I understand. A very wise rule." He smiled, and I couldn't help liking him.

"You are new to our community. If there is anything we at the church can do to help you, please don't hesitate to let us know. We have a children's club, an HIV support group—"

"We're not interested." Jabu shook her head.

"—and a community garden." Pastor Oscar ignored Jabu's rudeness. He never stopped smiling as he extended his hand once more. "I am glad to have met you. I will call again when your parents are home."

The three of us stood at the gate, watching as the pastor continued down the street. He paused to shake the hand of the sweets vendor on the corner and talk to the group outside the Community Chat. Solly opened the gate, and we went inside.

"You lied to a preacher," I whispered to Jabu.

"I had to." She locked the gate behind us. "I didn't want him to see how thin Baba is. He might get the wrong idea."

Or the right idea, I thought.

*   *   *

Sindi Skater flew across the ice. She arched her back and raised her free leg behind her, high over her hip, until she could grasp it with her hand and pull it over her head in the teardrop shape Mac called a Bielman position. I inhaled and felt the music flowing through me. Releasing my leg, I turned and glided backward in a long graceful spiral around the bottom of the rink. The ice was all that mattered, and a pair of silver blades was enough to let me fly like a bird.

As I turned forward, the lights went out in the rink. The huge ball they used to scatter colored light at parties swirled overhead in a confusion of blues and pinks and purples. Out of the darkness Kobus and Johann skated toward me. They were chanting, "You're gonna die! You're gonna die!" I tripped on my toe rake and crashed to the ice.

Mariki threw a rubber skate guard at me. "Get out of here before you infect us all!"

Even Lerato picked up balls of ice scrapings and threw them at me like snowballs in American books. Her mother pointed. "Your paint is peeling." But whether what she saw beneath was white or brown, I wasn't sure. The rink swirled and tipped dizzily beneath me. The cold crept up my arms to chill my whole body.

Nicola tossed her blond ponytail. She seemed undisturbed by the tipping of the ice. "No matter how good you think you are, you'll never be one of us." She skated to center ice and landed a perfect triple Axel.

Her mother's eyes blazed like the wicked queen in my old fairytale book. "Now *my* daughter will be the best skater of all," she cried. She began pushing me toward the entrance to the rink. The others joined her.

"Wipe that blood off your face and come back to class immediately," Liselle demanded, but she too pushed me toward the door.

I tried to scream. I wanted to cry out, "It's not my fault! I didn't do anything!" but no one listened, and I'm not sure any sound came from my throat.

I stood in the mall corridor outside, my nose pressed against the glass as I did when I was a very little girl begging my mother to sign me up for lessons. The music came through the glass, faint and far away. The skaters danced across the ice. They landed every jump. Every spin was perfectly centered. I wanted to jump and spin and glide too, but my feet felt as heavy as concrete. Inside, Liselle praised the skaters and said what a wonderful ice show it would be. Mrs. Brodowski clapped and told Mariki she had been chosen for the Junior Olympics. They never looked my way. They had forgotten I existed.

I pounded on the glass of the door. "Let me in!" I cried. Only MakaMboti smiled and waved and went back to serving hot chocolate and chips. Her son stared at me over her shoulder without smiling. He was thin as a skeleton.

* * *

I woke shivering. Michelle Kwan's smile was all that could be seen of the skating posters on the wall beside me. My pajamas were soaked with sweat, but my hands and feet felt as cold as ice. I got up quickly and backed away from the bed as though the nightmare were still tangled in the sheets and might reach out and grab me. Jabu sprawled in the other bed, her mouth open, snoring softly.

I tiptoed to the bathroom and washed my face with cold water. The house was so silent I could hear the ticking of the kitchen clock. It said nearly one. I got a glass of water and opened the back door to feel the breeze. It wasn't locked. I sat on the step while I drank my water. *It was just a dream,* I told myself, leaning against the doorframe so the cool night air could wash over me.

Something rustled by the back wall where Baba and Solly had started to build an extra room. It was supposed to be for Solly, now that he was almost a man. But they hadn't gotten very far before I left for Lake Placid, and now ...

A red spot glowed in the darkness. I rubbed my eyes, but the spot moved slowly like something alive.

"You couldn't sleep either," came Solly's voice from somewhere in the darkness. I stood and went closer. He flicked the ash of a cigarette into the scattered sand at his feet.

I sat beside him on the stack of unused cement blocks. The unfinished wall of Solly's room rose no higher than my knee, a monument to abandoned hope. "I had a bad dream."

"You wanna talk about it?"

The darkness settled around us so I couldn't see his face, only the red glow of the cigarette. I wondered when he had picked up smoking and if Mama and Baba knew. Radio music floating over the rooftops seemed to come from much further away than the *shebeen* in the next street. A dog barked. A car ground its gears.

"I dreamed that Baba had AIDS," I said into the darkness. Solly stiffened beside me. "In my dream they found out at the rink and wouldn't let me skate anymore. All I wanted was to float across the ice like a bird, but I was locked out."

Solly raised the cigarette to his lips again and drew in. He let it out in a long slow breath. The smell of tobacco made me want to cough.

"It was only a dream," Solly said in a flat voice that I didn't quite believe. "Go back to sleep."

Chapter 6

"I tried to call you yesterday," MakaLerato complained to my mother on the one day that week that she drove me to the rink. "A recording said the line was 'no longer in service'."

My fingers froze on my laces, and it had nothing to do with the temperature in the rink. No one was supposed to know we had moved to Tembisa. Too many questions with answers we didn't want to talk about. Slowly and deliberately I crossed one lace over the other and pulled them tight, waiting to hear what Mama would say.

Her laugh rang in the rafters. "Oh, we let the land line go. All mobiles these days, you know." MakaLerato laughed too and entered Mama's number in her mobile, but after that I took the taxi to the rink by myself.

Saturday morning I went to the library. Mama wouldn't let me walk alone even with the whistle she had given me to blow if I got into trouble. She sent Jabu with me.

"Sorry," I said when we were out the gate and Jabu was stuffing her whistle out of sight at the bottom of her purse. "I want to use the computer." We had never gotten around to signing up for Internet service when we left Kempton Park. I stopped asking when I figured out the real reason was money.

Jabu looked toward the corner where the Community Chat stood, but there was no one there. She shook her braids and squared her shoulders. "You had better not take too long."

When we reached the library, I went straight to the desk to sign up to use the computers. Jabu sauntered over to the long Formica tables where the community-college students studied. Every seat would have been taken during the week, since no one in Tembisa had any more study space at home than we did. But this was Saturday, and lots of tables were empty. Jabu settled at one and took out a sketch book and colored pencils. By the time I joined her, she was doodling beads and glossy starling feathers around the neck of an elegant black gown on a tall, slender fashion model. I sat on a hard chair beside her and took out my exercise book to finish some schoolwork while I waited for a computer.

I had to wait almost an hour. When it was time, I sat at a terminal wedged between a pillar and a magazine rack and went straight to Facebook. "Miss you!" Jenni wrote in a message. "Wish you were here." She posted pictures of camp that made me tear up, remembering all the friends I had made, thinking of what might have been if my father weren't so sick.

"Lithuania is awesome!" Ben said of his first stop on the Grand Prix tour. His new profile picture showed a bronze medal around his neck.

I sent Ben congratulations, and wrote back to Jenni to say I missed her too. I checked a few other Lake Placid friends, plus Lerato and Nicola. I sat a long time in front of the computer screen trying to decide what to post as my status. My American friends wouldn't understand about school here or what happened to Takalani. I couldn't write about home and how I felt about Baba being sick. "Feeling sore," I typed. "One day I'll get that double Axel."

My time was up; the next person stood over me impatiently. I logged out and pushed back my chair. Jabu's table wasn't empty anymore. Someone sat across from her. While I watched, he leaned forward and said something. I couldn't see Jabu's face, but she cocked her head in that coy way she sometimes had with boys she liked and I knew she was smiling. I wove between the bookcases and headed for the study tables. Jabu threw back her head and laughed.

"Shh!" someone hissed. Jabu hunched her shoulders like she was still laughing and leaned across the table to say something to the young man. He looked vaguely familiar. It was the guy outside the Community Chat when I first came home from America—the one flirting with the girl. I pursed my lips. James seemed to admire him, and anyone James admired was not someone I wanted my sister to hang out with. But then Solly knew him too. What had he called him? Makatso.

"Ready," I said as I approached the table.

Jabu flicked her hand at me. "Not now, Sindi. I'm busy. Go read a book."

The books in that section were all boring college textbooks. Makatso smirked at me and pretended to turn back to the open text in front of him. "Hotel Management" it said at the top of the page. He looked older than Jabu—too old if you asked me.

"Come on, Jabu. Let's go."

"Go on yourself! It's only a few blocks. It's not like you're a child. Besides, you have Mama's whistle." Her tone was disrespectful, and I didn't like it.

Makatso frowned. "A whistle?"

Jabu rolled her eyes. I pulled it from my shirt. "To blow if I get in trouble."

He howled with laughter. The librarian started in our direction with a frown on his face, and Jabu took a sudden interest in her fashion sketch.

When Jabu showed no sign of leaving, I walked out. I was pushing through the glass doors of the library when I heard my name. "Sindiswa! What are you doing here?"

"Mboti!" I gasped. What would Mboti's mother think if she found out I was at the Tembisa library instead of the one in Kempton Park? "Hi," I said and then couldn't think of anything else. "I haven't seen you in a while." His glossy brown cheeks were healthy looking, nothing like the skeleton in my dream.

"I'm working at my church these days," Mboti explained. "Wonderful Words of Life. I help with the children's club and the HIV support group. You know, visit the sick and stuff like that, be sure everyone is taken care of."

"Oh." An image of Takalani with blood streaming down her face came into my mind. Was anyone taking care of her?

"I … I have a friend," I began. She had acted like a friend to me, even if I hadn't defended her. Something in me wished I had. "Her name is Takalani. She's in my class at school."

Don't tell! Don't tell! ran through my head. I shouldn't be talking to Mboti. He would guess that I didn't live in Kempton Park any more. *Don't tell!*

But maybe I wanted to tell. Maybe I needed someone safe to talk to.

Maybe.

I chewed my lip and began again carefully choosing my words. "At least … she *was* in my class. She stopped coming after someone threw a rock at her." I touched my forehead above my left eye and glanced around to be sure no one was listening. "They said she had AIDS."

Mboti looked concerned. "Do you know where she lives?"

I looked across the street where the informal settlement began. "Somewhere over there, I think."

He nodded. "I visit several people in the settlement regularly. I'll ask around for her. Someone else in her family may be sick and she's taking care of them. Or she may be alone. There are a lot of child-headed households these day. Maybe we can help."

He talked so naturally that it seemed silly to keep HIV a secret. I stepped aside, out of the path of the people who came and went from the library. "That would be great," I said.

"How's your skating?" Mboti asked. "You went to America, didn't you?"

I grinned. America didn't have to be a secret. "I had a fabulous time. The coaching was great, and I made so many friends. I've got all my double jumps down except my Axel."

"Good for you." He raised his palm for me to slap, and I realized how much I missed seeing him every day at the rink. I slapped his hand, not caring what Nicola would say.

Mboti chuckled. "Frankly, I'm surprised you came back. I thought they'd keep you there, and we'd only see you on television."

I grinned. "Well …" I almost told him. It would have been so easy. He didn't work at the ice rink any more. But if I told him about Ms. Etherington and the scholarship, he would ask why I didn't stay. And then I would have to explain. And I couldn't.

It was a secret.

I tried on one of my mother's smiles. "I'd better go now. It was nice seeing you again." I started to turn away and then hesitated. "Um … Mboti?"

"Yes?"

"You won't tell anyone you saw me here, will you?" He wrinkled his brow in a puzzled expression. "I mean … your mother. She doesn't need to know. Or anyone else at the rink."

He looked at me and slowly shook his head. "Not if you don't want me to."

"Thanks, Mboti. You're a great friend." I started down the walk toward the gate.

"Let me walk you home," he said, coming after me.

"No! I'm fine. Really." He must have guessed I didn't live in Kempton Park anymore, but if I didn't show him the house, I could still pretend it was a secret. I left him standing on the walkway, library patrons flowing around him.

Maybe he'll run into Jabu in the library. I smiled to myself. I liked Mboti, and he had always had a crush on Jabu.

I didn't turn down our street at the church. Mboti might still be watching. Of course, I didn't look back to see, but just to be safe, I followed the road along the edge of the informal settlement. It stretched to my left as far as I could see. Thousands of people lived jammed together in that small space. I felt for the whistle around my neck. It *was* sort of comforting to know it was there although I would never tell Jabu that.

Little shops built of planks and recycled tin roofing faced the tarmac. They sold sweets and cool drinks and tiny boxes of toothpaste and washing powder—the kind that only cost a few rand, but you have to buy over and over instead of the big box Mama bought that cost more the first time but lasted a long time.

I slowed my pace and studied the customers at each shop as I passed. I hadn't meant to look for Takalani, but after a while I realized I was. She lived here—somewhere in the informal settlement. "Someone else in the family might be sick," Mboti had said. Is that why she hadn't come back to school? Was she taking care of a sick person—someone like Baba?

Then I saw her. She was standing at a kiosk a little way down an alley. She turned with a red cola can in her hand.

"Takalani!" I waved, but she started up the alley away from me without hearing. I ran after her. She turned into a side alley, and I followed along a piece of ground too low and boggy for even the shanty builders to use. Takalani turned again, and when I reached the intersection, she had disappeared. The path twisted and turned between tiny houses jammed together at odd angles. I picked my way around a pile of refuse and stepped over a smelly trickle making its way to the drainage ditch.

An old granny sat on a mat in the shadow of one of the shacks. A tiny girl with grubby pigtails that had grown out into a mat of fuzz sat motionless beside her.

"Excuse me, *Gogo*. A girl came by here just now. Did you see where she went?" The old woman looked at me from half-closed eyes and shook her head. I glanced around at the unfamiliar setting. Maybe I should turn back.

A couple boys about my age squatted nearby in the dirt. "What are you looking for?" one asked in a dreamy voice.

"James?" I blinked. His eyes were slightly glazed, and his companion had a bottle of glue in his hand.

James stood up. "Look who's here," he said slowly. He stumbled and grasped the weathered wood of a shack for support.

I backed away. "I was just looking for Takalani. She hasn't been in class for a while, and I thought maybe I'd visit her and make sure everything is okay." I knew I was babbling, but I couldn't stop.

The other boy stood, slipping the glue bottle into a ragged pocket. He was taller than James and looked older. "Sure. We know where she is."

I stared at him as he came near. He smelled as if he bathed in the drainage ditch or not at all. "That's all right," I managed to say despite the dryness of my mouth. "I … I'll find her later."

I turned to flee up the alley, but the boy grabbed my arm and held it in an iron grip. James laughed, a hard humorless laugh.

"We'll take you to see …" The taller boy turned to James. "What was her name again?"

"Takalani."

"Yeah. Takalani. She's a good friend of ours. We know right where she is." He pulled me toward him, and I wriggled, trying to free my arm, but his fingers dug deeply into the muscle.

James crowded close and hissed in my ear. "Come along, Sindi, and you won't get hurt." His rancid breath in my face choked me.

"Maybe another day." I glanced over my shoulder at the old woman. "I don't need to find her right now." My breath came in short, fearful gasps.

The *gogo* waved an arm at the two of them. "You bad boys get out of here. Leave that girl alone," she said in the *isiXhosa* tribal language.

The older boy laughed and said something insulting to her—something no one should ever say to an old person—and the boys pushed me up the narrow track between shacks. The *gogo* shouted after them, and her mouth was as foul as theirs.

"We'll take you there right now," the boy said.

"No! I don't want to go!"

James laughed again, and the sound grated on my ears.

I tried to pull away, but they half carried me toward a gap in the shacks with the weedy bank of the ditch beyond. The whistle! I needed to blow the whistle Mama had hung around my neck, but I couldn't reach it. I dug the heels of my tackies into the dirt. "Stop it! Let go of me!" But they only pulled harder.

We were between the shacks now. The ground plunged steeply down toward murky water. I had been pulling back. If I suddenly threw myself forward, it would surprise them, pull them off balance. They might let go.

I looked at the water and gagged. At least it was flowing and not completely stagnant. But last night's heavy rain had left plastic containers and torn shopping bags caught in the weeds at the edge. The body of some dead animal buzzed with flies. The smell made me want to vomit.

Or maybe it was fear. Even falling into that water would be better than what James and his friend planned.

I suddenly shifted my weight and sprang forward with all the strength of a triple jump. As I suspected, the boys, who had been dragging me in that direction, couldn't stop the movement. With a cry, they let go, and we all three plunged into the ditch.

Chapter 7

My mouth filled with the putrid water of the drainage ditch. It came up along with my lunch as soon as my head broke the surface.

"Sindiswa!"

James thrashed and shouted curses beside me. The ditch wasn't deep. I tried to stand, but slipped on the slimy bottom and lost my footing.

"Sindiswa!" Someone was calling my name, high pitched and frightened.

The boys splashed across and climbed the opposite bank, disappearing into another part of the settlement.

"Sindi! Here! Take my hand." Mboti stood just above the water line. He held one hand out to me and with the other gripped a scrawny shrub that clung to the bank.

"Mboti!"

He dragged me from the water, and I fell, sobbing, in his arms, as safe as Solly's or Baba's. We lay on the bank while my body shook uncontrollably.

The *gogo*'s voice in *isiXhosa* came from above. "I told that girl not to go with boys like that. It's her own fault. Foolish child. No wonder we got so much of that AIDS when this is the way they behave. Yoh, when I was a girl in Transkei ..."

I buried my face in Mboti's shoulder. I could hear the thumping of his heart through his T-shirt.

"It's all right, Sindi. She's just frightened for you. It was her shouts that helped me find you."

I rolled off him to vomit some more in the weeds. "You followed me."

He didn't deny it. "Come on. I'll take you home."

I crawled up the muddy bank on my hands and knees. Mboti helped me to my feet. I didn't dare raise my head and look at the people who had gathered to see the excitement. Where were they when I needed their help? I sniffed and wiped slime from my face. As Mboti led me limping away, I glanced back. A face looked at me from the crowd, a thin, anxious face with a fresh red scar over her left eyebrow—Takalani.

"Mboti!" I clutched at his arm. "There she is! Takalani."

He turned to look. "Where?" But the face was gone.

* * *

We stopped at the public tap on a tiny square of broken concrete in a packed-earth courtyard. Mboti borrowed a container to draw water and wash the worst of the muck from my face and hair and clothes. I just wanted to go home and stand in the shower. Would I ever feel clean?

The women and girls waiting their turn to draw water watched silently or murmured among themselves. Whether they knew or guessed what had happened, they didn't ask questions. Mboti poured water in his hand and tried to wash the front of his T-shirt where I had laid my slimy head. It didn't help much.

"Thank you," Mboti told the lady who had lent him her container.

I shivered in spite of the warm spring day. My tackies squelched as we walked away. No one spoke to us. I didn't know if they stared or not; I didn't raise my head until we were almost home.

"Hello, Jabulile," Mboti said.

My head jerked up. Jabu was coming toward us with the guy from the library—Makatso. It seemed to take her a moment to recognize Mboti, but when she did all the laughter drained out of her face. She glanced at me and back at him. "Mboti! What are you doing here?"

"Just making sure Sindi gets home all right. She had a bit of an accident."

Makatso sniffed. "What happened to you? Go swimming in a drainage ditch?"

"I fell in."

Jabu wrinkled her nose as she picked a twig off my damp T-shirt.

"Mboti pulled me out," I continued, not daring to tell her how much more he had rescued me from.

She raised those dark eyes of hers to Mboti and for a moment I thought she might say something nice, but then she was once again my bossy older sister. "You'd better get cleaned up before Mama comes back from shopping and sees you."

She glanced over her shoulder as she hurried me through our gate. "You idiot!" she hissed in my ear. "Now he knows where we live."

"He won't tell."

"How do you know?" Her grip pinched my arm.

"I asked him not to."

Jabu rolled her eyes at me and shoved me through the front door.

* * *

We were careful not to wake Baba. Jabu shut herself in our room. I crept into the bathroom and locked the door. When I had stripped, I stood in the shower with hot water running over me. I soaped my body and shampooed my hair. Then I rinsed and did it all over again. I didn't stop until the hot water ran out, and I shivered from the chill.

I wrapped myself in a soft towel and sat on the toilet lid. A stench rose from the heap of clothes on the floor. I wrapped the towel around me like a sarong and carried the clothes at arm's length to the bin by the back door. Then I emptied all the bins in the house over the clothes and went back to the bathroom to scrub my hands and arms in the cold water.

Chapter 8

When I stepped on the ice Monday morning, I couldn't relax. "Come on, Sindi! Focus!" I murmured.

I did crossovers around the end, a serpentine pattern through the middle of the ice, and turned backward to do the same thing coming the other way. I dodged Liselle and Kobus practicing loop jumps and avoided Mariki, whose music was playing on the CD player. You didn't get in Mariki's way when she was running through her program. You didn't get in Mariki's way *any* time if you could help it, but especially not when she was practicing for a show or a competition. I did back twizzles around the end of the ice and started on power threes.

Thump! I caught my toe rake and went down. I got quickly to my feet, clutching my hip, and kept skating. Liselle looked my way. *Ignore the pain,* I told myself. *You must always keep skating.* I breathed deeply. Already it didn't hurt so much. Liselle turned back to Kobus.

I was rushing. My mind was only half at the ice rink. The other half—I stumbled on an easy turn and nearly fell again. *Don't think about the settlement. Don't think about facing James at school today. Think about skating. Think about flying over the ice like a bird.*

Nervous thoughts gnawed my stomach like rats on a sack of mealies. The ice blurred, and I sniffed loudly, but I moved so quickly past the other skaters that I didn't think anyone would notice.

"Look out!" Lerato's call echoed in the rafters too late for me to stop. I crashed into Mariki, and we both sprawled on the ice.

"What do you think you're doing?" she screamed. She used a lot of Afrikaans words they didn't teach in school.

"I'm sorry," I murmured, rubbing my elbow. "I didn't mean to …"

"Mariki, Mariki!" Mrs. Brodowski skated over to us. "Are you all right?" She took Mariki's skate blade in her hand and pulled her leg out to stretch the muscles and keep them from cramping. Mariki gripped her knee and whimpered. It wasn't a that-hurts-but-I-don't-want-to-be-a-baby-and-cry whimper. It was a pay-attention-to-me-because-I'm-the-most-important whimper.

"Really, Sindiswa!" Mrs. Brodowski went on. "You must keep your eyes open. Mariki had the right-of-way. What were you thinking?"

"I'm sorry," I murmured again.

"Are you all right?" Liselle laid a hand on my shoulder. I nodded. She sent Kobus off to practice his loop. "Let's begin with some stroking," she said. "That'll settle you down."

We did edges for a while—backward, forward, inside, outside. Usually edges calmed me with the precision they required, but today my heart wouldn't stop fluttering. It showed. Everything felt rushed and sloppy.

Liselle looked at me with concern. "You mustn't worry about Mariki, Sindi. She didn't mean those things she said. You know how high strung she is."

I shook my head. "I'm not worried about Mariki."

"Then what's wrong?"

I should have let her think I was worried about Mariki.

"Everything okay at home?"

Don't tell!

I nodded dumbly. Was it a lie if you didn't open your mouth?

Liselle waited. "You aren't concerned about the ice show, are you? You'll do just fine. You know this program; you've trained for it; you're ready. And you have that beautiful dress from the States." She smiled.

I nodded and looked away. Could I trust her? I needed to talk to someone about what had happened on Saturday. Not Jabu. She'd blame me. I needed to tell someone how worried I was about my father. Not Mama. She had too much to worry about already.

"It's just …" I began.

Don't tell! Don't tell!

I stopped and fixed my eyes on the ice at my feet.

"It's just what?" Liselle asked. When I didn't answer, she glanced at the stands. I think she would have talked to my mother if she had seen her. For once I was glad Mama wasn't there.

I shook my head again and took a deep breath like a swimmer coming up from under water. "Nothing. I'm fine."

Liselle sighed. "Let's see the opening of your program then. Without the music."

* * *

I lingered by the school gate until the last minute just as Takalani used to do. *Maybe James won't turn around,* I told myself as I slid into my seat behind him. *Maybe he won't see me.*

The bell rang.

James turned around.

I pretended to be busy looking for something in my satchel.

He studied me intently. "Did I see you …?" he began, and then stopped as though confused.

I bent over my satchel and thrust my hand to the bottom, ignoring him as best I could.

"Weren't you …?" he began again.

Miss Diniso stood in the front of the room. "Today we will be discussing the value of nutrition and exercise for preserving good health," she began. "Sindiswa?"

I stopped rummaging in my satchel and folded my hands on my desk. "Yes, miss."

"Class has started. Pay attention."

"Yes, miss."

James snorted.

Miss Diniso glared at him. "James, you will face front."

He gave me one last smirk before he turned around. I stared at my exercise book. Miss Diniso's voice echoed in some distant place that had nothing to do with me. Maybe James was too high on glue fumes on Saturday. Maybe he didn't remember the drainage ditch. Slowly the beating of my heart returned to a normal pace. Maybe.

Chapter 9

Jabu tried to hang out with Makatso at the Community Chat on the corner. Mama wouldn't hear of it.

"Solly does," Jabu insisted.

"Solly is a young man," Mama replied. "It's different for young men." But she didn't explain why. I didn't want Jabu hanging out with Makatso, but it didn't sound fair to me to have different rules for girls and boys.

I watched Solly from our gate. He leaned on the wall next to Makatso with a cigarette in his hand. Solly punched James in a playful way like they were buddies. Thabo was there too, but he seemed to be on the edge, like he wanted desperately to belong, but wasn't quite sure he did. I wished Solly didn't.

Jabu came out the gate and grabbed my arm. "Come on, Sindi. Let's go to the library."

"The library?"

"Yeah. I told Mama we were going."

She gazed over her shoulder toward the Community Chat as she steered me up the street. When she turned back, she wore a sticky sweet smile. Makatso dropped his cigarette, said something to Solly and the others, and came slowly after us.

"Jabu! What are you doing?" I asked.

"You want to use the computer, don't you?"

"Sure, but—"

"So let's go to the library." She didn't look back anymore, but I wasn't surprised when Makatso joined us shortly after we had settled at the study tables. I left them to take my place at the computer.

Jenni posted beautiful pictures of the autumn leaves in the mountains near Lake Placid. Funny to think of it being fall there when it was spring in South Africa. She was working on her novice test. Ben won gold at his second competition and qualified for the Junior Grand Prix final in December. Nicola tagged Lerato and me in the pictures she posted of the three of us making funny faces into the camera, and several of my Lake

Placid friends commented. Even Mac. He sent a private message saying he hoped my father would be better soon. I didn't know what to say so I deleted it.

* * *

We went to the library a lot that spring. I didn't complain. I really did want to use the computer, and Mama was reluctant to let me go alone. But she didn't know about Makatso. I almost told her when Jabu and Makatso took to slipping out. But I didn't. Jabu trusted me to keep the secret.

"Just getting a breath of fresh air," Jabu said the first time. "It's so stuffy in here."

I couldn't deny that. Summer was coming, and the library's air conditioning couldn't keep up. I didn't trust Makatso, but it was almost my turn at the computer. I watched them go. They had barely passed through the security system when he laid his hand on her back. *She should push him away,* I thought. But she didn't.

Usually they were back by the time my turn was up on the computer, Makatso with his sly grin, Jabu focusing intently on her book as though they had been there the whole time. Usually.

One afternoon in November I plopped myself in the plastic chair in front of the computer and logged into Facebook. I hadn't posted anything in more than a month. I was becoming a lurker, but I had to know what Jenni and the others were doing. How else could I imagine what life would be like when I took up Ms. Etherington's offer? Someday. Maybe. If she didn't change her mind and sponsor someone else instead. I sighed.

I hadn't been online in a couple days, and there were three messages, all from Jenni.

"Sindi! What are you doing keeping secrets from me???"

My heart froze. The sounds of the library grew muffled in my ears. I blinked twice and squinted to see the screen.

"Dad just let it slip that someone asked him about you staying with us and training at Lake Placid."

I let out my breath slowly. Wrong secret.

Jenni's message continued, "(He won't say who, but I think I can guess. Ms. Etherington sponsors Ben, and he says she asked lots of questions about you last summer.) But why didn't you tell me??? Why didn't you stay???"

I sat back and pursed my lips. *I didn't stay because my family needed me. I didn't stay because if my father is going to die ....* I blinked back tears. I could just delete Jenni's messages like I did Mac's. A click of my finger and it would go away. I wouldn't have to check Facebook ever again. But I didn't delete. I scrolled down to the second message.

"Sindi!!! Where are you??? It's not the same without you here. Everyone is so boring and ordinary. I would love to have you stay with us. We have an extra bedroom if you don't want to share with me."

How could Jenni think I wouldn't want to share her beautiful pink and white bedroom? The room I shared with Jabu could fit in it four times over. And besides—Jenni was my friend.

I scrolled to the last message, sent late last night. "Are you mad at me?" she wrote. "Why don't you write? I'm sorry if I hurt your feelings in some way. I didn't mean to. I really liked skating with you and having you for a friend. I hope you'll come back. You don't have to stay with us if you don't want to."

I had hurt her feelings. Nothing could be more wonderful than to share Jenni's room, go to school with her, tell secrets at night, and skate every day with her and the others. But now she would be angry with me, and it was all because of the stupid secret. Enough of secrets.

I clicked reply. "Sorry I didn't answer sooner. I'm not mad at you, Jenni. I couldn't stay in Lake Placid because my father has ..."

I stopped and stared across the bookcases at the empty place at the study tables where Jabu and Makatso had been when I sat down at the computer. They weren't there. Taking "a break" again no doubt. I wished I knew what they did on those breaks.

No. I didn't want to know. I just wanted my sister to be smart and safe. It didn't take a medical degree to know Makatso *wasn't* safe.

The computer screen drew me back. I couldn't tell Jenni the truth. I couldn't betray my family. I backspaced. "Because my father is sick," I typed slowly and deliberately. "My family needs me." I sent the message before I could change my mind and left the computer even though I still had twenty minutes left in my time slot.

I went outside to wait for Jabu. The evening breeze evaporated the sweat from my skin while I sat on the low wall that edged the walk. Andile rounded the corner in front of the library. I looked around for a way to make myself invisible. Andile did odds and ends at the ice rink. He and Mboti used to mop the whole arena on Mondays and Fridays and empty all the dustbins after ice hockey games. Andile had taken over some of Mboti's duties in the pro shop, but he drove the Zamboni too fast over the ice and missed spots. The ice was never as smooth as when Mboti used to do it.

What if Andile comes here? I couldn't let him see me—not here in Tembisa. He wouldn't keep my secret. According to Nicola, he was the one who reported seeing Mboti coming out of the AIDS clinic. Some friend. I got up slowly and edged toward the shadows of the building.

But Andile didn't turn into the library. He stopped abruptly, frowned, and crossed to the far side of the street. He never looked back as I craned my neck to watch.

"Hi, Sindi." Mboti came up the walk.

"Hi," I said, suddenly realizing why Andile had crossed the street.

"You all right?" Mboti asked.

I nodded. "I just saw Andile."

"Oh." He sat on the wall and patted the space beside him. I sat. "Did he see you?" Mboti asked.

"No."

"That's good then. Right?"

"I thought he was your friend."

Mboti was quiet for a long time.

"Was that legal for them to fire you?" I asked.

He shrugged. "They said I was late and not doing my job effectively."

"Late? Andile's the one we always have to wait for to open up in the morning."

Mboti nodded. "I could have fought it, but I had to think about my mother."

"You mean they could make an excuse to fire her as well?"

"They could. And then where would we be?"

"It's not fair. It's not fair for you to lose your job. It's not fair for Andile to cross the street and pretend he doesn't see you." *It's not fair for me to be burdened with a secret that builds walls between me and my friends.* I didn't say it out loud, but the unfairness pressed behind my eyes and made them sting.

"A lot of things aren't fair," Mboti said quietly.

I watched an ant crawling along a crack in the paving stones. "It is true?"

"Is what true?"

"What they said … that you have AIDS?" I couldn't look at him when I said that word.

"It's true that I have HIV in my blood," he said without pause. "The disease is controlled by medications."

I took a deep breath and watched the people coming and going from the library. I didn't look at Mboti when I said, "My father's a lot better since he started taking medications."

"I'm glad," Mboti replied, and there was a smile in his voice. "How is your mother?"

I gave him a quick look. This wasn't telling the secret, was it? Not exactly. I let my breath out slowly. "She takes a lot of 'vitamins'. She says everyone can use a boost to the immune system. But … she doesn't share her 'vitamins' with the rest of the family."

Mboti chuckled. "Your parents need to know you're there for them no matter what, that you love them, that you aren't judging them. It's the stigma that makes it so hard for us to talk about … things like this."

I think he almost said something different, but I hadn't really told him the secret, so he couldn't use those words.

His voice was gentle. "The fear of being embarrassed, losing friends, or losing a job keeps people from getting help until it's too late."

His eyes looked over my shoulder. I turned to see Jabu and Makatso pause outside the gate. Makatso ran his hands along her bare arms. I looked at Mboti. His jaw clenched. *He cares.* When I looked back at my sister, she wore that sultry look you saw on TV. An unnamed fear stuck in my throat, and I tried to swallow.

Jabu turned into the library yard, and Makatso continued down the street with a cocky tilt to his chin that made me want to smack him. A pleased little smile curled Jabu's lips as she floated up the walk.

Mboti stood. "Hello, Jabulile."

Jabu started as though she hadn't been aware of us there. "Hello, Mboti." She smiled pleasantly. Where was my snappy sister?

Something sparkled on her wrist. "What's that?" I demanded.

Jabu extended her slender brown arm to admire the bracelet of white and gold beads. "It was a present. Nice, isn't it?"

It was. But Makatso wasn't nice. I craned my neck to look around her, but he had disappeared in the crowd of workers returning home at the end of the day. "Why did he give you that?"

"Sindi!" Jabu frowned and pulled her wrist back, wrapping it protectively with her other hand. "I think it's time we went home." She whirled around and started for the gate.

"Goodbye," Mboti called as I followed.

* * *

Jabu didn't speak to me that evening. She shut herself in our room. "Mama! I need some privacy," she complained when I tried to go in. Solly went to get his inline skates. "Mama!" Jabu called.

I sat on the love seat in the lounge with Baba and watched television—a local talent show. Boys dressed in skins did a traditional dance, kicking their feet high in the air to the beat of a drum.

I drew Baba's arm around my shoulders and nestled into the hollow of his arm as I always had done. He was better—lots better since he started taking the medications. Maybe I had been wrong to think he had AIDS. Maybe he would be completely well soon and I could go to New York.

"Could you kick that high when you were a boy, Baba?" I asked.

He waved his hand dismissively. "These city boys don't dance. Why, I kicked higher than my head. I loved dancing like you love skating." His face glowed with pleasure at the memory.

"I wish you could show me."

Baba laughed. "I'm too old for that now," he said, but I knew that wasn't the only reason.

I wished I had shown an interest in his childhood before he got sick, when he might have shown me how high he could kick, when his stomping could make the seed pods tied around his ankles rattle with the rhythm.

Baba ran his fingers along my arm and shook his head. "I should have had that test a long time ago."

I swallowed hard. His hair had turned gray and reminded me of Nicola's grandfather who used to come to all our competitions and shows before he died of a heart attack last year. I didn't like to think of my father as an old man like Nicola's grandfather.

"You will come to my ice show, won't you?" I said.

"Of course I will, Nyoni."

Chapter 10

The next day when I logged onto Facebook, there was a new message from Jenni. "I'm sorry your father is sick. It's not cancer or anything serious like that, is it?"

"No, it's not cancer," I typed back. I wished I could tell her the truth.

Before I could read anyone else's post a reply popped up. "Hi, Sindi!!! I'm so glad it isn't anything serious. I hope your father gets better soon. So why can't you come back to Lake Placid and stay with me? Please, please, please!!! You're too good to quit skating."

Jenni was online in Lake Placid. What time was it there? She must be checking from her phone on her lunch break.

"I haven't quit skating," I typed back. "We're doing an ice show in a few weeks. I'm skating the *Out-of-Africa* program."

"Awesome!!!"

We typed back and forth for a few minutes across the miles. It wasn't the same as giggling in the locker room, but for those few minutes I was back in Lake Placid where all that mattered was landing the next jump, sharing the moment with my friends. In my love for skating I could almost forget the secret that weighed me down. Then Jenni brought me back to reality.

"Didn't you tell me that none of the coaches there is as good as Mac?" she wrote. "I still think you should come. You have to follow your dreams!!!"

Dreams. Americans talked a lot about dreams. They didn't know about losing jobs or HIV or how shame crushed hope. They were all about one person—"the individual," they called it. They didn't bother much with community and responsibility for others.

The next person stood over me, waiting his turn. "I can't. Gotta go," I typed and left the library.

* * *

A week later it stopped. "Aren't we going to the library?" I asked.

"No." Jabu lay across her bed, her face buried in a fashion magazine.

"No?"

"You heard me." She wasn't wearing the beaded bracelet she had been showing off to everyone who would look at it.

I sat on the corner of my bed. "I guess you and Makatso broke up."

She turned a page without looking at me. "Makatso is a jerk and a liar, and I don't ever want to see him again."

But I didn't believe her.

* * *

I was in the kitchen, helping Mama chop greens to cook in peanut sauce for dinner.

"Nicola has a new skating bag," I ventured as casually as I could manage. "It has a metal frame you can use for a seat if there isn't a bench around. Jenni had the same kind at Lake Placid. Lots of the girls did, actually."

Mama didn't say anything.

"They're very practical," I added. "I was wondering …" I hesitated. "… if maybe I could get one like it."

"You have a skating bag." Mama handed me an onion to chop.

"Maybe for Christmas," I prompted. "My old one's getting pretty beat up. I had trouble with the zipper the other day, and the wheels get stuck."

Mama sliced the greens into tiny streamers.

"Mama?"

She jerked her head up as if I had startled her.

"I said, maybe I could get a bag like Nicola's for Christmas."

She turned back to the greens. "You can have your baba's old suitcase—the roller bag he used to take on trips to Cape Town."

"Mama! That looks like ..." I couldn't be disrespectful of Baba. "It looks like it belongs to someone who works for the Ministry of Finance," I finished. "Please can't I have a new bag? I won't ask for anything else for Christmas."

She grunted and attacked the greens with her knife. "If your baba insists on paying school fees for the children of his no-good brothers in Kwa-Zulu again, there won't be any Christmas for his own children this year."

I stared at her. I had never heard my mother talk this way.

But she didn't stop. "I'm the only one bringing in a salary anymore, and I would think I should have some say." She pursed her lips and chopped vigorously. I dumped my onion in the pot and turned on the gas fire without looking at her.

They must have been arguing before Mama came out of the bedroom and said Baba needed to rest. I guess I picked a bad time to bring up a new skating bag.

I added some oil to the pot and stirred. Of course, Baba was expected to help the rest of the family with school fees. The older relatives had sacrificed to send him to school; now he was responsible for the younger members of the family. That was the way it worked. The teachers couldn't let learners study for free. They needed to eat. Baba's illness made no difference to that. I looked at Mama. Had they even told the family he wasn't working anymore? How far did this keeping of secrets go?

Mama reached into the cupboard and pulled out the peanut-butter jar. She opened it and stared inside. "Solly!" But Solly was off somewhere with his inline skates and not there to explain why the sides of the jar were scraped nearly clean.

"I'll get some more," I said, turning down the burner for the pan of onions.

There was a shop not far away. I wasn't sorry to get out of the kitchen with Mama in this mood. My steps slowed when I noticed Thabo leaning against the red metal wall of the Community Chat. A cigarette dangled from his fingers just like Makatso. James huddled by the container with a skinny man whose jeans looked like they were about to fall off. The man glanced around before taking something from James's hand and moving off. They didn't seem concerned that I had seen their drug deal.

I crossed to the other side of the street. Maybe James and Thabo wouldn't notice me. But one of them whistled. Heat rushed to my cheeks. I kept walking without turning to look, but their shouts and laughter followed me until the road curved out of sight.

I came back with the peanut butter by another street that approached the Community Chat from the back. Jabu and Makatso stood on the weedy path in the shadows behind the container.

"Please, Makatso! We've got to talk." Jabu was saying as I approached.

Makatso frowned and turned away. "There's nothing to talk about."

I stopped. If I came closer, they might see me. I should have walked on the far side of the street. What was I thinking?

Jabu grabbed Makatso's arm. "But what if I'm—"

He shrugged her off, his handsome face twisted in a sneer. "That's not my problem. You're a child, Jabu. You're not ready for a real relationship." He towered over her, and she looked small and vulnerable next to him.

I was at her side before I gave myself time to think. "You leave my sister alone!"

Jabu stared at me. "Sindi! What are you doing here?" There was a note of panic in her voice. "Are you spying on me?"

"No!"

Makatso laughed. "The little lioness is defending you, Jabu. I hear she goes swimming in drainage ditches too."

My stomach clutched, and I swallowed hard. Now I was the one who needed defending. James and Thabo rounded the corner of the container and stood, arms crossed, watching the spectacle. I fell back a step as if I had been pushed, then caught myself and stood my ground.

Makatso laughed again. "Go on, Jabu. Go play with that goody-goody the little lioness hangs out with." His voice grew soft and seductive. "What's his name? Mboti? You know he wants you." Makatso made an obscene gesture before he turned his back and walked away.

Jabu drew back her arm and hurled something after him. It hit him squarely in the back before it fell to the dust. Gold and white beads glittered in the late afternoon sun.

"Come on, Sindi. Let's get out of here." Jabu pulled me up the street behind her. When I glanced back, James was picking up the bracelet from the path. He handed it to Makatso, who slid it into his pocket. They gazed after us with matching sneers.

Chapter 11

"Close your eyes."

I held very still while Jabu edged my lids with black liner that Mama would never let me wear except for the ice show. "There. Now … how about some of this?" She brushed my cheeks with a fat stick that left silver glitter behind.

When she was done, I smiled at my reflection in the mirror and shook the braids Jabu had woven so tightly. They swooped over my scalp in tight patterns before cascading to my shoulders. Each braid ended in a pattern of pink and gold beads that matched the skating dress that hung in its nylon garment bag from a hook on the door.

I had never been so excited. Baba was well enough to come just as he promised. He would see me skate the program that had won the gold medal at Lake Placid.

"Now hurry," Jabu said. "It's almost time to go."

"I'm coming. I just want some aspirin." She left, and I rummaged in the medicine cabinet, but the aspirin wasn't there. *Maybe it's by Baba's bed.*

The others were talking in the lounge as I darted into Mama and Baba's room. Several bottles stood on the night table, and I picked one up. "Leah Khumalo" the prescription label said. "Take with food twice daily at seven AM and seven PM." "Leah," not "Everest." The label gave the name of the medication. It wasn't vitamins. It was one of the medications they had mentioned at school for HIV. I couldn't pretend anymore that I didn't know. They both had it.

My hand trembled as I returned the bottle to the table.

"Sindi! Are you coming?" Jabu called.

* * *

We parked further from the entrance to the mall than we needed to at this hour when most of the shops were closing.

Hardly anyone would walk past our car in this spot.

"Sindi won't be on before seven-thirty at the earliest," Mama told Baba. Although he was stronger than he had been in weeks, he didn't move from the passenger seat. Solly leaned forward from the back to listen. "Probably closer to eight o'clock," Mama said. "Jabu will send you a message from her mobile."

Solly nodded and held up Baba's phone to show he was ready.

"Can't Baba come in?" I begged.

"I told you, Sindi, he'll get too tired if he comes for the whole show," Mama said. She turned and started walking toward the mall entrance.

Jabu clenched my hand. "Do you really want your friends to see the way he has aged?" she hissed in my ear.

I sucked in my breath. His thin face and gray hair would surely give away the secret. "No," I whispered. I raised my hand to wave.

"Good luck, kid!" Solly called after us.

When we reached the arena, Andile took the CD of my music and checked it off his list. "Good luck." He smiled.

"Thank you," I mumbled, wishing it were Mboti, who had run the sound system for as long as I could remember.

We left Jabu spreading a blanket to save seats on a bench with a good view of the ice. When Mama and I got to the dressing room, it was crowded with skaters and their mothers. Mariki examined her makeup in the mirror and used a delicate finger to smooth the edges of her lipstick. Nicola and I looked at each other and giggled. Johann van der Walt from the Pretoria club would be on the program.

I stepped into the soft pink dress and pulled it up over my shoulders.

"Ooh!" Lerato let out a long sigh. "It's beautiful." She touched the beads and sequins one after the other with her long brown finger.

Nicola's mother frowned. "Where did you get a dress like that?"

"It was a gift," I said as Mama tucked in the neckline. "From someone in the States."

"Humph. Too bad it wasn't someone rich enough to sponsor your training." Mrs. Brodowski turned her back and interested herself in adjusting the angel wings on a small skater or she might have seen the guilty look on my face.

"It was a lovely gift," Liselle said, arranging the chiffon skirt. "We need a picture."

"Yes, Mama, please! Take a picture of Liselle and me so I can post it on Facebook."

"Let me get my phone." Mama opened her handbag. A half sandwich in plastic wrap sat on top. "Take with food," the pill bottle had said. I glanced at the wall clock. Almost seven.

Lerato's mother laughed at the sight of the sandwich. "You were afraid you might get hungry? Let me tell you, Leah, the kiosk has great meat pies. Not healthy, I must admit, but very tasty."

Mama laughed too and glanced at the clock.

They told us about anti-retroviral drugs at school—ARVs—about how important it was to take them at the same time every day or the virus would mutate and the medicine wouldn't work anymore. I glanced again at the clock, but I couldn't imagine Mama taking her pills in front of all these people—not without someone—probably MakaLerato—asking questions.

Mama held up her phone. "Smile."

The smile on my face felt stiff and fake as Mama snapped the picture. All I could think of was the sandwich in her bag and the pills she needed to take at seven.

MakaLerato adjusted the orange feathers woven into her daughter's hair. "What a shame Everest couldn't be here." Her voice asked a question even if her words didn't. The other mothers stopped what they were doing and looked our way.

Mama didn't hesitate. "Yes. It *is* a shame, isn't it? Lerato, come over here and let me get a picture of you with Sindi." No one but Lerato moved. Mama would not get off so easily. "Everest had to be away on business," she said as she arranged Lerato and me in front of the skating-club bulletin board and snapped our picture. "Cape Town. You know how it is." She gave a nervous laugh.

"Over the weekend?" Mariki's mother's neatly plucked eyebrows went up.

"Terrible, isn't it?" Mama answered as she put away the phone.

* * *

Nervousness sent me to the toilet one last time before the show started. From behind the closed door of the last stall, I heard Mariki's mother talking to Kobus's stepmom.

"I don't understand what kind of father would miss his daughter's ice show for a business trip to Cape Town." I kept very still and hoped they wouldn't notice my feet beneath the door of the toilet. "You would have thought he could plan better, or at least fly home for the weekend."

Kobus's stepmom clicked her disapproval. "And I haven't seen Leah at practice in ages. Such a talented daughter, but her mother shows no interest in her career."

I wanted to charge out of the toilet, beat them on their chests, and scream at them. "You don't understand! You don't know!" But I drew my feet back into the shadows of the toilet. I didn't come out until they had gone.

* * *

The arena was full when the show started. Seven o'clock had come and gone. Had Mama taken her pills? Not when I was looking. Maybe when I was in the toilet?

The learn-to-skate classes skated up and down and made circles to "Jingle Bells." Christmas was near, although there would be no sleigh rides in the snow on this side of the world. In Nicola's solo she fell hard on her Lutz jump. She got up, her smile tense with pain, but she glanced at her mother and kept skating. Mrs. Brodowski frowned, but she didn't yell as she would have in practice. Lerato's spin combination was the best I had ever seen it. I wished she could come to skating camp with me at Lake Placid. She would love Jenni and Ben and the others.

I picked nervously at the pink beads in the lace of my dress. What if I fell? I knew in my heart that Baba wouldn't be here for next year's show. No one else mattered. Only skating for him. I glanced over my shoulder toward the door. Where were Baba and Solly? The program showed only one more skater, and then I would warm up with the last group.

I turned to Jabu. "Did you send the SMS?"

She nodded and glanced toward the entrance.

What if it was too far for Baba to walk from the car park? Maybe he wasn't as strong as I had been telling myself. What if they were late and missed my skating? I blinked several times and clapped for Kobus's loop. He did a spread eagle around the bottom of the rink and came back up the ice for his last spin.

"We will have a brief intermission while the final skaters warm up," said Nicola's father on the loudspeaker when Kobus had finished and the clapping stopped.

"Let's see how you look." Jabu turned me round. "Perfect," she said, adjusting the skirt of my dress and letting her fingers linger on the fabric.

I kept twisting around to watch the door, but there was no sign of Baba or Solly. Mama took my face in both her hands. "They'll come, Sindi-wam. Now go." She turned me toward the ice and patted my bum.

I stepped on behind Mariki and the senior ladies champion who had come all the way from Cape Town. Johann van der Walt was right behind me. He and Mariki had been making eyes at each other all evening. I stroked down the ice and did fast crossovers around the end. I watched the door as I stretched my free leg in a long, steady spiral. No Solly. No Baba. When I turned backward, I couldn't see the door anymore.

Don't think about it, Sindi Khumalo. He'll come. He promised. I didn't let myself look at the entrance for the rest of the warm up, but my boots felt as heavy as bricks. My spins wobbled, and my jumps hardly left the ground.

Liselle stood by the barrier when I came off. She smiled. "Don't be nervous, Sindi. You'll do fine." But her face was tight, and I knew she was worried.

I had only a minute to catch my breath as the other skaters left the ice. I glanced at the rink entrance and back at Mama. Her smile looked stiff, as if she was as disappointed as I was. Jabu looked grim until she saw me watching her and forced a smile. I wanted to cry.

Liselle turned me toward the ice and squeezed my shoulders for reassurance.

"Ladies and gentlemen," said the loudspeaker, "please welcome Kempton Park's own Sindiswa Khumalo."

Liselle pushed me forward. I blinked back tears and stepped onto the ice. *A champion never stops skating,* Mac always said. I straightened my shoulders, spread my arms wide, and took my starting position. I looked one last time toward the door.

Something was happening. People were moving away to make space for someone coming in, someone with grey hair and wrapped in a heavy coat. Solly was with him. A bag, heavy with skates, seemed to fall from my shoulders. My chin came up, and my face relaxed in a smile. I felt as if I could jump into the rafters.

Baba was here!

The music started. Mac probably thought Kenya was right next door to South Africa when he chose *Out of Africa.* The distance didn't matter. The music bubbled up inside me like fizz in a cool-drink bottle. It sparkled to my fingertips like the beads and sequins on my dress. *Oh Baba, I love you! Just for one more night I want you to know my joy!* My spiral sequence swooped and glided like a swallow. My double loop floated into the atmosphere and landed soft as a feather. My feet danced, and my spins exploded with excitement. I searched the crowd by the entrance doors to be sure he was really there. I had to know that he could see me and that he knew I was skating just for him.

He was there.

I swept across the ice in graceful curves and stopped in the center with a grand flourish. Everyone was on their feet, clapping and cheering as if I had won that Olympic medal I dreamed of. Mama and the other African ladies made their piercing, ululating cries. Kobus whistled as loudly as Ben. Liselle jumped up and down and clapped with excitement. I could hardly breathe.

Over the heads of them all, from far out on the ice, I saw my father clap and wave. Then he and Solly slipped back out of the door and were gone.

Chapter 12

MakaLerato was hugging my mother as I stepped off the ice. "We'll have to tell Everest what he missed," she gushed. "That child of yours is incredible!"

Liselle practically lifted me off the ground with her hug. "Sindi! You were marvelous! We have to find a way to send you back to Lake Placid to train again next winter."

My breath caught in my throat. I knew there was a way.

Liselle swung me around. "We're going all the way to the Olympics someday. I just know it."

I smiled, but I could hardly think of the Olympics. Right now the most important thing was that my father had seen me skate even better than at Lake Placid.

I nestled contentedly on the bench between Mama and Jabu. MakaMboti waved and gave me a thumbs up from the kiosk. I waved back. I was sorry that Mboti hadn't been here to see me. I watched Mariki and Johann and the other champions skate from inside my own bubble of joy.

"No more lessons until after Christmas," Liselle reminded us when the show was over. "But the ice will still be here. It's a good idea to keep training on your own so you don't lose those spins and jumps!"

Most of the skaters, their families, and their guests had already gone by the time we came out of the arena into the mall corridor. MakaLerato and my mother talked and laughed as they always used to do at practice. Lerato's father discussed marketing and investments, or something boring like that, with Kobus's father while Kobus and his stepmom walked ahead.

"You skated really well," Lerato said.

Jabu agreed. "Even that Mariki what's-her-name wasn't as good as you."

A warm glow filled my whole body. "Thanks." How I wished I could go back to Lake Placid and really train.

Our voices echoed in the empty mall along with the clip of our shoes on the floor. The security gratings were lowered over the closed shops. Only a few people came and went from the restaurants and cinema. The ladies passed a planter and headed for the entrance. Lerato's father followed with Kobus and his parents.

A couple slid out from the shadow of the planter and sauntered toward us. The young man had his arm around the girl's slender waist, and his face bent over hers to steal a kiss. Or maybe he was looking down the front of the skimpy top she wore. He could probably see a lot. The girl tossed back her head and laughed.

It was Pretty Mogane, the girl from my class who had mocked me for skating. "Hello, Sindiswa," she said when she saw me. "Still hanging out with white girls?" She only said that to hurt. Lerato and Jabu were as dark-skinned as I was.

But when she spoke, the man looked up. Jabu drew in her breath sharply beside me. "Makatso!"

For just an instant, Makatso looked frightened. Then his eyes turned hard and mocking. Pretty laughed and brushed her body against him. A bracelet of gold and white beads sparkled on her wrist.

"What will that sugar daddy who pays your school fees say?" I blurted.

Pretty ran her fingers down Makatso's jaw as they kept walking. "What he doesn't know won't hurt him." But that wasn't true. What he didn't know could kill him, or at least change his life forever.

Lerato shifted uncomfortably. "Let's go."

But Jabu wasn't listening. She glared at Makatso. Her jaw was set, and her eyes focused into tiny points like the sun through a magnifying glass that we once used to burn paper in a science experiment. I thought they might burn right through Makatso's shirt, but he guided Pretty into the out-of-the-way corner by the entrance to the toilets and went on laughing and whispering as if we weren't there. Jabu took a step toward them.

"Jabu ..." I didn't think she heard me.

The laughter stopped. "What are you looking at?" Pretty demanded. Makatso turned around, his eyes carefully veiled.

"You are disgusting," Jabu said to him.

He glanced nervously around as though he was scared a security guard might hear.

Jabu turned to Pretty. "What kind of lies has he been telling you? Has he mentioned the great discounts he gets at the travel agency where he works?" Her words were light and friendly with an edge as sharp as broken glass. "I'll bet he suggested a trip to Cape Town. Or maybe a romantic getaway to Mauritius." The girl jerked her head up, and I knew that he had.

Jabu took another step forward, and Makatso pressed himself against the wall. "Did you ask him how many other girls have worn that bracelet on your wrist? Believe me, it's not worth the price you paid for it. Dump him. He's only lying to get what he wants. He's not worth it."

She tossed her head and marched back to me. "Makatso, we need to talk sometime," she flung over her shoulder. "Come on, Sindi. Let's go home."

Lerato skittered after us.

*   *   *

Solly disappeared into the back yard as soon as we stopped in the carport. He had been stiff and silent on the drive. Baba seemed to have shrunk as small as Sindi Skater in his big coat. He went straight to bed. I didn't like the way he coughed.

"Why do you need to talk to Makatso?" I asked as soon as Jabu and I were alone in our room. "I thought you hated him."

She looked at me sharply. "I do hate him." She turned away and hung my skating dress in the wardrobe.

"So? It's over, isn't it?" I demanded.

She stood there with her back to me. "It's never really over," she said into the wardrobe. Nothing more. I guess I was still the little sister.

I put on my pajamas and crawled into bed, feeling as limp as the impatiens in Mama's garden when I forgot to water them. Jabu pulled her shirt over her head and tossed it in the corner. She slipped her jeans over her hips and stopped. Her panties had a bright red spot on them. She pulled her jeans back up and sat abruptly on the edge of the bed. Trembling, she covered her face with both hands. They slid down and pressed against her mouth while she blinked several times. Even in the dimness of the overhead light, I could see tears sparkling in the corners of her eyes.

"Are you all right?" I asked softly.

Jabu stood up. "Go to sleep." She took a tampon from the drawer in the wardrobe and went to the bathroom.

So that was why she wanted to talk to Makatso. But now it was truly over, wasn't it? No. If Jabu was worried about being pregnant, then maybe they hadn't used protection. I curled into a ball and pressed my arms into my stomach. It hadn't ached like this a few minutes ago. Even condoms fail; I knew that much. But if they hadn't used protection, there was more than a baby to worry about.

The sound of water running from the bathroom drowned the sound of Baba's dry cough in the other room.

* * *

I must have fallen asleep because sometime in the night I woke. Jabu's bed was empty. Unfamiliar voices came from the lounge. I threw off the covers, tiptoed to the door in my bare feet, and opened it in time to hear the front door close. "Mama?"

She was dressed as if she was going out although it had to be past midnight. Jabu stood beside Solly, a frown on her face.

"Mama, where are you going?"

"Hospital. It's Baba's chest again."

I grabbed Mama's sleeve. "Is he ...?"

"Sindi-wam." Mama put her hands on my shoulders and squeezed. "Please, I must go now. I'll be with him. Go back to

bed and get your sleep. You can visit tomorrow, I promise."
She gave me one of her strong looks.

The blue lights of the departing ambulance flashed across
the walls of the lounge. It was my fault. He wasn't strong enough,
but I had begged him to come to my ice show. Why did I do it?

Mama picked up her handbag and fished for her car keys.
"You children should all go back to bed." She pulled out the
keys. The half sandwich in plastic wrap and a little packet of pills
fell to the floor. Mama swept them up in a quick gesture and
stuffed them back into her handbag. She fiddled with the clasp
and avoided our eyes.

How many times had Mama missed taking her ARVs—I
mean, her "vitamins"? How often could a person miss and still be safe?

"I'm going with you," Jabu announced. She pushed
Solly's foam mattress aside and sat on the loveseat to buckle her
sandals. Solly stood in the corner. His eyes darted here and there
like a frightened springbok, ready to flee if Mama asked *him* to go.

"That's not necessary," she said. "You need your sleep."

Jabu opened the front door and waited for Mama to pass
through. For a moment the secret that no one would talk about
hung between them.

"Very well," Mama said at last, "but Sindi and Solly
should be in bed."

I knew I wouldn't sleep.

Chapter 13

The next day, just before noon, Mama and Jabu came and got us. Mama parked the car in the lot outside the hospital complex. We joined the queue waiting for the gate to open and visiting hours to begin. I wanted to ask if Baba would be all right, but I didn't dare.

The sun was hot on my skin, and a trickle of sweat slid over my cheek and dripped from my chin. People spilled from taxis and came to join us. They spoke with quiet dignified voices, not like the crowds waiting to get into a soccer match or socializing after church. Solly stood by Mama and tried to protect her from getting squashed, but when the gate opened and the crowd spread out in different directions, he hung back.

"Are you coming?" Jabu demanded.

"Yeah." Solly shuffled after us, but he glanced around as if he would rather be anywhere else. I slid my hand into his. He gave me a grim smile and walked a little faster.

The crowd flowed down a neatly swept cement walkway shaded by a corrugated roof past long, brick buildings. Bright hollyhocks grew tall against their walls, smiling the lie that everything was just fine.

It will be all right, I told myself. *Baba will be better today.* But the smell of antiseptic slapped me in the face as we entered the ward, and my skin prickled with fear. It was Solly who squeezed my hand and drew me on.

A dozen men in clean striped pajamas sat in their beds and looked expectantly toward the door. I scanned their faces but didn't see my father. Beyond them was another room and another, all open to the bright nursing corridor where we walked in a row behind Mama, pretending we didn't see the lines of beds with dark faces looking our way—looking for someone to tell them it would be all right.

"This way," Mama said. She showed us to a smaller room on the other side of the passage. There were only two beds here instead of twelve. The smell of flowers and fresh-cut grass drifted through the open window along with the murmur of visitors passing back and forth on the shaded walkway.

"Baba!" I said and leapt forward.

His eyes smiled at me, but he didn't say anything. He couldn't. A fat, plastic tube filled his mouth. My stomach clenched as my eyes followed its length to a machine that whooshed in rhythm with the rise and fall of his chest. My own chest heaved. I couldn't seem to get my breath. I clutched the rail of his white metal bed. Was I going to faint? Right here in the hospital?

No. The dizziness passed.

I had intended to thank my father for coming to my ice show. He would smile, and we would talk about last night. He would be better. That was what I had told myself. That's the way it was supposed to be. Not …

I love you, Baba. I love you! Please get well. Please, please, please! The words cried out inside me, but I couldn't say them. If I opened my mouth, I knew sobs would come instead. Sindi Skater, who had seemed as big as the whole arena last night, had shriveled as small as a raisin in the heel of my shoe. I leaned on the side of the white metal bed and took Baba's thin, dry hand.

The man in the other bed curled on his side and faced away. A nursing sister pulled the curtain between the beds.

"Mrs. Khumalo, may I see you outside for a moment?" she asked. Mama followed her.

"I love you, Baba," Jabu said. Her voice was tight, but she got the words out. All I could do was nod and sniff. Jabu took Baba's other hand. I think he squeezed it. He squeezed mine. He looked at Jabu, and he looked at me. I longed to hear him call me "Nyoni" one last time.

His eyes are saying it, I told myself, *even though his lips can't.* Then his eyes slid past me to Solly in the doorway.

Solly stood very still. He stared at Baba with hard, angry eyes while a little muscle jerked up and down in his cheek. Baba's eyes were soft and wet, and you could tell there was something he was trying to say to Solly. He squeezed my hand with the effort until I wanted to pull it away and rub it, but I didn't. I just pressed my lips together and bit down until they hurt and I forgot about my hand.

I didn't know if Solly understood or not. For a moment I thought he did. He raised his chin and blinked several times. Then he turned away and left the room. He bumped into Mama in the doorway.

"Where are you going?" she asked. "Solomon Khumalo, I'm talking to you."

But Solly didn't stop.

Chapter 14

The next day Solly didn't come in with us. He waited at one of the little cement tables in the grass between the hospital buildings. Baba was sleeping and didn't wake up even when I called his name. But he squeezed my hand just a little. At least, I thought he did.

Baba died on Tuesday, in that hospital room surrounded by strangers. I wasn't there. Nobody who loved him was there. We were home in our beds, thinking, "Tomorrow we'll see him. Tomorrow he'll be better."

But he wasn't.

We didn't go to school that week. Mama didn't exactly tell us we could stay home. We just did, and she didn't say anything about it. Pastor Oscar came. And Mboti. Neighbors came and went and brought food. Somehow they seemed to know.

On Friday we drove behind the hired mortuary car to KwaZulu-Natal to the homestead where Baba grew up. We used to visit his mother, our *gogo*, there during the summer holidays. The traditional beehive house that Gogo always insisted was cooler in summer had been allowed to fall down since she died. Its woven reeds lay in a sad heap.

Our Uncle Njabulo lived in a cement-block house on the compound that was as nice as our brick house in Tembisa. Uncle Thulani's house, almost as nice, faced it across the earthen yard.

The men carried Baba's coffin up the steps of Uncle Njabulo's house.

"Careful there!" Uncle ordered. "Don't gouge the wall!"

Mama stiffened beside me. I don't think she liked Uncle Njabulo any more than I did. He disapproved of her "independent, city ways."

Uncle Thulani didn't try to help the men maneuver the coffin through the narrow doorway. He sat in the shade near the cattle kraal, looking as thin and frail as Baba had.

He has it too, I realized when I saw him. A shudder ran through me.

His wife, Thokozile, brought him a cup of tea. Her head was bowed, and she bobbed a little curtsy to him, but he didn't make her kneel like Uncle Njabulo did when Auntie Zanele served him. I knew it was just the traditional way of showing respect, but I never saw him kneel to anyone.

Auntie Thokozile dragged her feet through the dust toward the summer kitchen. There was no little one tied to her back with a bright cloth as there had been when we were here last summer. Just before we moved to Tembisa, Uncle Thulani had called to say that the baby had died. Six months old and never any bigger than a newborn. "Thokozile" meant "happiness," but my aunt didn't look happy to me.

I know why the baby died, I thought. *Where will it end?*

"Where's Bongiwe?" Jabu asked, glancing around the earthen yard for the cousin nearest our age.

Some of the little outbuildings had thatched roofs, some had corrugated zinc. They served as extra rooms for the older cousins or to store things, just as Baba and Solly had intended to build at our house.

Only at our house it had never happened. I tried to swallow the lump in my throat.

"There," I said. Bongiwe looked out at us from the shelter of the summer kitchen. I gave a little wave. Her fingers moved slightly before she turned back to stir a large pot over the fire.

"Come along," Mama said, and we followed her into the house. One of the bedrooms had been emptied. The men settled the coffin on a table in the middle of the room and went out. Auntie Zanele spread a new plush blanket over the closed top as if she were tucking my father in for the night.

Mama dropped onto one of the thin mattresses along the wall. Auntie Zanele went out and returned with another blanket to wrap around Mama, but Mama shook her head. "It's too hot!"

Auntie Zanele drew back. I wasn't sure if she was shocked or angry that Mama wasn't following custom. Mama sighed and reached for the blanket. "Very well. Thank you."

The windows of Uncle Njabulo's house were smeared with white ash, announcing the death in our family. Neighbors came and went. They sat and drank tea, ate biscuits, and talked quietly. No one questioned us when we told them Baba died of pneumonia. No one asked why the medicines didn't save him. Not aloud.

People I barely knew came to offer their respects. Many were relatives, but we saw them so seldom that I didn't remember their names. I looked at the floor and nodded politely even though I could barely hear their whispered condolences.

Most of the women wandered round to the back of the house where big iron pots simmered over glowing fires. I could hear the rhythmic thump of mealies being pounded for pap and occasionally muffled laughter as the women responded to some story. My cousin Bongiwe and the others were with the women, but Mama and Jabu and I weren't allowed to help. Solly sat with the men outside where they talked in low voices.

When it began to get dark, Bongiwe brought candles. Someone I didn't recognize brought us plates of food and plastic tumblers of filtered water, and still we sat.

"I need to go to the toilet," I whispered to Jabu. It wasn't a flush one like in the city, but a new pit had been dug with a fresh cane screen around it. I knew where it was, but I wasn't anxious to go alone in the dark. Jabu sighed like she was impatient with me, but it was only from habit. I knew she was as tired of sitting on the floor in this stuffy room as I was.

"Come on," she said. She whispered something to Mama, who nodded and went back to talking with Baba's cousin. Uncle Njabulo came to the door as we left and motioned to Mama.

As we stepped outside, a breeze blew up the valley and licked at my sweaty skin. A million stars glittered across the eastern sky. They were stars like we never saw in Jozi. Sindi Skater burst out of my shoe and soared to meet them before I thought to hold her back.

Jabu must have felt the same joy rising in her soul. "Wouldn't I like to design a dress made of that," she breathed beside me.

I slipped my arm through hers. "And I'll wear it to skate," I whispered.

I had been longing for the ice since Baba died. Slow, quiet, heartbreaking music played in my head. My back arched until it ached, and my leg raised high over my head as I glided on the long graceful curves of my mind. In the real world my feet stumbled over each other, forgetting that tackies on ground didn't move like blades on ice.

Jabu caught me, but for once she didn't scold.

We found the cane enclosure and did what we had come for. When we returned to the house, I paused on the step, reluctant to go back into the stuffy house.

"Everest died of pneumonia." My mother's voice came from around the corner of the house. "He did not die of witchcraft."

Witchcraft? I stared at Jabu. "Who would think—" I started to whisper, but Jabu put a finger to her lips.

I couldn't see Uncle Njabulo's flabby face, but I recognized his voice. "Then the *sangoma* will tell us as much," he said.

I swiveled around to look at Jabu. *The sangoma!* We both knew we shouldn't listen, but she drew me with her into the shadows of the lounge with its single candle.

"But we are Christians!" my mother sputtered out of sight.

"What does that have to do with it?" Uncle Njabulo insisted. "We are Zulu. I am the head of this family now." His voice was proud, and I wondered if he had been jealous of my father. "My brother neglected the ancestors far too long. They must be very angry. Remember, it is not just your husband who has died."

Uncle Njabulo didn't believe anyone died of natural causes. I thought of my baby cousin whose short life was so full of pain and of Uncle Thulani, thin with sickness. To Uncle Njabulo even the cows giving less milk would be proof that the ancestors were angry. His chair creaked as he got to his feet. "The *sangoma* is coming Sunday afternoon," he said. "You will be ready."

"Sunday?" Mama squeaked.

Jabu's face was grim. Even I knew these things were not usually done so soon after a death. Surely Uncle should wait until after the mourning—long enough for us to be far away in Jozi.

"We really should start for home on Sunday," Mama said in a nervous rush. "The children have school on Monday."

"Their father has died," Uncle Njabulo said harshly. "They will be excused from school. The *sangoma* will discover for us whose witchcraft caused the pneumonia, who weakened him so that a strong man like my brother succumbed to this disease."

I felt for Jabu's hand in the darkness. I knew what had weakened him, and it wasn't witchcraft.

"If you had nothing to do with this," Uncle continued, "then you have nothing to fear."

"Me?" Mama gasped. "How can you even think that I—"

Uncle's voice dropped to where we could barely hear him. "Or perhaps *you* gave him the disease—the sickness that weakens the blood and wastes the body."

Silence descended on the house like a smothering wool blanket. Jabu pushed me toward the room where Baba's coffin sat on the table, covered with the plush blanket. We hardly looked up when Mama came in and dropped onto her mattress. I wished we hadn't heard.

* * *

Sometime after midnight I fell asleep leaning against Jabu's shoulder. I woke stiff and uncomfortable.

"It's time," she said. The lightening sky showed pale through the ash-covered window, but I could hear people beginning to move around. I went to relieve myself and wash in a basin of cold water.

When all was ready, Uncle Njabulo, Uncle Thulani and some other men took the handles of the coffin. It was a fancy one from the city, not locally made, and Uncle Njabulo had a little smile of pride on his face as he rubbed a speck of dust from the brass work.

I know that many people are buried in cemeteries these days even in the countryside, but Uncle Njabulo was very traditional. The grave had been dug along the top of the cattle kraal within sight of the house. It was a good thing it wasn't far, or I don't think Uncle Thulani could have managed. He looked exhausted.

Mama wasn't allowed to come near because she wasn't born in the family and might hex the cows, or something like that. She stood with the aunts off to the side where Gogo was buried since she wasn't born in the family either. Auntie Zanele's blanket was still wrapped around Mama's shoulders. Auntie Thokozile wailed aloud, and I wondered if she was crying for our father or for her own loss or if she was just angry at Death, who refused to leave us alone.

Mama pulled the blanket over her head. She cried so hard that Auntie Zanele practically had to carry her. I looked back over my shoulder at where they stood under the tree and wished someone had given me a blanket to cry under. Jabu wailed and leaned on Bongiwe. I clung to them and sobs shook my shoulders. The same thoughts kept attacking my mind. If Baba hadn't come to my ice show, he might still be alive. He wasn't strong enough, but I had begged him to come.

Someone began a hymn. At the sound of the music Sindi Skater slipped from my heel and glided across the surface of my mind. She didn't jump or spin; she soared gracefully as a bird and swooped low over the soil of my father's grave. Nyoni.

The words of the hymn were all about heaven and Jesus making a way. It was supposed to be hopeful and comforting, but I didn't want my father to be in heaven; I wanted him here with me. I clenched my teeth and stuffed Sindi Skater firmly back where she belonged. Solly's hand touched my shoulder, and I turned to him. He was tall and strong as Baba used to be, and he held me and let me cry. Once in a while I felt his body shake as if he was crying too.

When the pastor had said the words, the men pushed sand into the hole until it was full. We went back toward the house and the feast the women had prepared. Along the way, we stopped to wash our hands in a pottery bowl. When all had washed, Uncle Njabulo struck the bowl with a spade. It shattered into a dozen pieces that lay in a puddle of spilled water and damp earth. It was finished.

Chapter 15

As I left the latrine Sunday morning, I came upon Mama and Uncle Njabulo. "This afternoon," he said, gripping her arm. "You will be there."

She raised her chin and for a moment looked him in the eye. Then she saw me over his shoulder, lowered her eyes and nodded submissively. Uncle dropped her arm. "City whore," he spat.

I gasped and took two steps toward them. *How dare he—*

"Sindiswa," Mama called. "It's almost time for church. Hurry and get ready." Her eyes warned me to do nothing.

"Yes, Mama."

She rubbed her wrist where Uncle had gripped it and turned away.

* * *

Mama drove us to the Baptist chapel on the ridge. "We are not traipsing through the mud to sit for hours in the sun with those so-called Apostles shouting and carrying on," she insisted as Uncle Njabulo and the rest of the family headed for their place of worship by the river. I think if she could have figured out a way to get our things in the car without Uncle Njabulo seeing, Mama would have driven straight on to Jozi.

But she didn't.

After church we ate leftover boiled meat and the rest of the scones from the funeral feast. I wasn't very hungry.

The *sangoma* came in the afternoon. Most *izangoma* are women, but this one was a man. Except he didn't look like a man. He wore a beaded headband and masses of beaded braids that came almost to his waist. His build was slight like a woman's too, and he was wrapped in skins and red, white, and black cloths.

"He's very good at talking to the spirits of the ancestors," my cousin Bongiwe said. "He found Baba's lost cattle, and when Auntie's baby died, he sacrificed a chicken so no one else would get sick."

I stole a look at Uncle Thulani and thought the dead chicken hadn't done much good.

The *sangoma* wore a necklace of bones and teeth and feathers, so maybe he was a healer as well. When he turned around, I saw the small, dry, goat bladder from the feast at his initiation as a *sangoma*. It looked like a little balloon among all the beads of his braided hair.

"Don't stare," Jabu whispered and nudged me, but the children were all staring. I'd never seen a real *sangoma* before. As Mama said, we were Christians. Zulu was just the language our family spoke and the place we went for holidays and funerals. The kids at school teased me about my accent and called me "coconut" because my skin was dark but inside I was more like a white person. Maybe they were right.

The *sangoma* and his two assistants sat with our two uncles on a mat under the biggest tree in the yard. Auntie Zanele didn't offer them anything to eat as she would ordinary guests. Eating our food might weaken the ancestor's spirits. At least, that was what Bongiwe said.

Jabu went behind the house and helped Bongiwe with the washing up.

"I'll look out for the children," I called after her, hoping for a chance to peek around the house. It was easy to keep the little ones from going near and bothering the grownups; they were as frightened of the *sangoma* as I was. It was strange that he came here. I thought usually people went to see him. Maybe Uncle Njabulo wanted to be sure Mama wouldn't have an excuse to stay away.

At last Uncle motioned to Auntie Zanele, and she called the family together. We approached silently—Uncle Njabulo's eight children; Uncle Thulani and Auntie Thokozile with her children trying to hide behind their mother's skirts from the awe-inspiring sight of the *sangoma*; an old man that Uncle Njabulo said was Grandfather's youngest brother; and Mama, Jabu, Solly, and me.

"We are gathered to determine who caused the death of our brother Everest," Uncle Njabulo said.

Solly's eyes flicked suspiciously between the *sangoma* and our uncle. Jabu's were wide and anxious as if she feared some revelation from the fortuneteller. Mama stood with quiet dignity as though the *sangoma* wasn't even there. Uncle Njabulo introduced each member of the family. We knelt in turn in front of the *sangoma* and put our hands together to show our respect. When it was Mama's turn she hesitated, and I thought she was going to refuse, but she knelt. *It's not worship*, I reminded myself. *It's only the Zulu way to show respect as Uncle Njabulo's wife and children do to him.* When Mama rose, her jaw was set and her eyes shot fire.

When the introductions were done, Uncle Njabulo motioned to my cousin and me. "Bongiwe, Sindiswa, you will take the children to the other side of the compound and keep them there out of sight. This is adult business and none of your concern."

Bongiwe knelt and accepted his command. I took the hands of little ones and led them toward the house. I glanced back once. Jabu was staring at the ground at her feet. I felt guilty to escape when she couldn't, but she had nothing to fear. I was the one who had begged Baba to come to my ice show. That was why he got sick again. What if the *sangoma* figured out that it was my fault? Maybe if I wasn't there when he cast the bones, he wouldn't know. But I felt his eyes on my back as I left. Perhaps he already knew.

* * *

It wasn't easy to keep the younger children on the far side of the compound. Bongiwe's little brothers seemed to think it was a game to see if they could escape us and run around the house. After kneeling in front of the *sangoma*, being within sight did not seem quite so frightening as it had before. At least they did it silently, and I didn't think they drew the attention of the *sangoma*, casting his bones and entering his trance. Someone beat a drum in a slow steady rhythm.

The boys stopped their game when Uncle Njabulo's young daughter-in-law scolded them. She wasn't much older than Jabu, but she was a married woman with a new baby—a son—

and that earned her respect. She had come away with us on account of nursing the baby. She looked healthy, and so did her husband, but you couldn't tell by looking if someone had HIV. Would their baby join his cousin and the ancestors in the field behind the house?

The drumming continued for a long time. Bongiwe took the older ones to the fields to shoot birds with their catapults, and I helped her sister-in-law to look after the babies. At last the drumming stopped. The mothers and aunties returned silently. Jabu came to the tap in the yard and washed the sweat from her face and arms.

"What happened?" I whispered.

She shook her head. "I don't want to talk about it."

"But did they find out who killed Baba?" My voice squeaked with tension.

Jabu turned on me. "Nobody killed Baba," she said. "He died of pneumonia."

"Is that what the *sangoma* said?"

She looked across the compound to the tree and shook her head. "Inconclusive. He wants to come back tomorrow and do a bigger ceremony with dancing at night."

"Tomorrow?"

Jabu wiped her hands on her skirt. "Stop worrying. He might decide it's one of the ancestors who's angry, as Uncle Njabulo said. Then they'll kill a chicken, and it'll be messy, but it'll be done. Harmony between the living and the dead and all that."

I shivered and turned away.

Chapter 16

At night Jabu and I sweat together in one small bed in one of the extra huts, but instead of sleep, there was only the dream of hospital smells, echoing corridors, and the steady drumming of the *sangoma*.

Mama woke us early in the morning. "Get up. We're leaving," she whispered. "Quietly now. We don't want to disturb the rest of the family." I suspected it was Uncle Njabulo she didn't want to disturb. He would make us wait for the return of the *sangoma*.

I glanced at Bongiwe and two of her little sisters asleep on a foam mat on the floor as I gathered my things. I dressed in the cane enclosure where we washed. The morning was cool, but the cloudless blue of the sky promised that it wouldn't stay that way.

Auntie Zanele was up. I thought that would spoil Mama's plan to get away without an argument, but she looked relieved. Auntie served us tea and fresh mealie porridge under the avocado tree. Uncle Njabulo's bakkie was missing from its parking place under the bedroom window.

"Where is Uncle Njabulo?" I asked.

"He went out early on business," Auntie Zanele explained. So that was why Mama was relieved. He wasn't even here. He must have left very early, for the sun was not yet over the hills, but my aunt didn't say anything more.

Mama took a deep breath. "You must give him our regrets and express our appreciation for his hospitality these last few days, but I think it is time my family returned to our own home. It has been a difficult week, and the sooner the children are back in their usual routine, the better."

Auntie nodded and bowed in acceptance of Mama's words even though we all knew it was only an excuse. "I will prepare food for your journey. *eGoli* is far." She used the *isiZulu* name for Johannesburg—Place of Gold. She rose from her knees.

"That isn't necessary," Mama said. "There are places to stop along the way."

"But *Sisi*, I would be a poor hostess if I let you travel with nothing to sustain you." She began sorting through a pile of pots and pans still draining on a wooden rack outside the kitchen shed.

"No, sister. There is no need. There is meat left from the funeral. We will take some of that with a little fruit. It is enough."

My aunt nodded. "You will take meat and fruit, but it would be shame on me and our house to send you without bread, and the muffins and scones are gone."

She roused Bongiwe to go to the shop for more baking powder. "I'm afraid I used it all on Saturday," she apologized.

"Really, that's not necessary," Mama said.

"But it is," Auntie insisted. "I need more anyway. Bongiwe, be sure she gives you a fresh box—not something that has been sitting on the shelf for months."

"*Yebo*, Ma."

Jabu and I walked to the shop with Bongiwe. She led us up a steep path that cut off a long loop of the dirt road. The shop was nothing more than a few boards nailed together to make a shanty in someone's compound. It took several minutes of calling and banging on the gate before a girl came out yawning and opened the long window that hung over the fence to form a counter. Inside were shelves of salt and spice, toothpaste and stomach medicine, cans of warm cool drink and bags of sweets. There was barely room for the girl.

As we walked back along the road to the top of the steep path with our tin of powder, I looked down into the valley. The sun glistened from the roof of Uncle Njabulo's house, standing in the midst of the other farm buildings. At the top of the cattle kraal a rectangle of newly turned earth showed dark against the dry earth—my father's grave.

When we got back to the farm with the baking powder, Auntie mixed it with flour, eggs, and a lump of butter she had made herself. She poured in a little cow's milk from a jug and stirred the scones. It seemed to take forever to find the right pan, heat the oven in the house, and bake the scones.

Mama glanced at her watch. "I really had hoped to be home by lunch time, but now …"

I think she was also worrying that Uncle Njabulo would return from his business and try to stop our going, but he didn't come. What business could be so urgent that it had to be done so soon after his brother's funeral?

We finally left a little before nine. It took twenty minutes to reach the tarred road although it hadn't taken so long to walk it with Bongiwe. But the road was rough and rutted. The car couldn't go any faster than we could have walked. It wound several hundred meters to the south to avoid the steep bank we had climbed on foot. I stared through the car window. A swallow dipped and swooped and rose again into the sky over the farm as Sindi Skater had swooped and soared during the funeral. "Stay with him, *nyoni*," I whispered. "Stay with my *baba* for me."

It was ten before we reached a road where Mama could actually drive at the speed limit. We ate the scones with slices of cold beef as the green hills of KwaZulu gave way to the yellow grasslands of Mpumulanga.

We had hardly said a word. Occasionally Jabu consulted the map and said something to Mama about how far it was to the place we needed to turn off. Solly crouched in his corner, listening to music on his earphones.

"What day is it?" I asked suddenly.

"Monday," Mama answered.

"No, I mean what day of the month?"

Jabu calculated. "Must be ten December."

"That's what I thought." I turned to Solly. "Yesterday was your birthday and we forgot."

Solly shrugged. "No big deal."

"But it is!" I insisted.

Solly laughed through his nose. "Congratulations, Solomon. You're the man of the house."

Mama frowned in the mirror.

Solly put his earphones back in and stared out the window. I settled back in my corner and looked out my side. Little houses dotted the green hills or clustered in towns on the yellow plain. I let my mind drift to that private place where Sindi Skater was free to glide and soar, leap and spin.

Solly had the music turned up so loud that I could hear it faintly even without his earphones. It beat a powerful rhythm like the *sangoma's* drums, and Sindi Skater jumped and did fast footwork in time to it. But even in my imagination her feet got tangled. I couldn't make them go right. The edge slipped from under her, her arms flailed awkwardly, and she crashed to the ice.

I pinched my lips together. This was silly. I closed my eyes and focused. Inside, inside, toe rake, jump! But even as the skater in my mind rose into the air, I knew that the flip was tilted too far. She came down on two blades, ankles still crossed, and collapsed in a heap. I squeezed my arms over my chest and hunkered down in my corner. Could not even my fantasies go right? I stared out of the window and silently counted backward from a thousand to drown the sound of Solly's music.

Chapter 17

We were hot and tired by the time we reached Jozi. The traffic robots were out in Tembisa. It hadn't rained in weeks so someone must have stolen the electric cable again. Without the signal, vehicles moved slowly through the intersection, and I had time to watch the people coming and going from the church on the corner. Pastor Oscar stood outside a big shipping container along one wall. He seemed to be directing the women who walked back and forth, carrying sacks of maize meal or beans on their heads to a bakkie parked by the church. Mboti supervised the loading.

"Almost home," Mama said as she turned into our street. Jabu's head swiveled to watch the group outside the Community Chat. Pretty Mogane leaned against Makatso. James and Thabo passed a cigarette back and forth between them.

"Scandalous," Mama said as she pulled into the entrance to our drive and stopped. Solly jumped out with the gate key in his hand, but he didn't need the key. The gate stood ajar, and as Solly swung it open, we all gasped. There in the drive stood a bakkie, its back piled high with furniture—our furniture.

"Great God in heaven, what's happening?" Mama exclaimed. A man who looked vaguely familiar tossed an armload of clothes over the side of the bakkie onto the cushions of our loveseat. He glanced at the open gate with no sign of concern, and then called something toward the house.

"That's my best blouse!" Jabu shouted. She leaped from the car and darted into the yard without bothering to close the car door.

"Jabu!" Mama screamed. She turned off the car and ran after her.

I sat in the middle of the back seat and stared. The bakkie had KZN license plates—KwaZulu-Natal. An ugly fear began to grow in my stomach.

Jabu ran to the bakkie, pulled an armload of clothes from the back and threw them onto our bit of lawn. "What do you think you're doing?" she screamed at the man who had put them in the lorry.

Uncle Njabulo appeared in the door of the house with a pile of folded blankets and the cover from my parents' bed. So this was his urgent business. Mama ran at him yelling and waving her arms. All that submissive-Zulu-woman thing was gone. Solly hesitated a moment before following her into the yard. Makatso and Pretty stared in the gate with a growing crowd.

"Excuse me," I said as I climbed out and shut the car door carefully behind me. "Excuse me." I pushed past James and Thabo.

Jabu reached into the back of the bakkie and drew out a bundle of jeans. The man with Uncle Njabulo reached for them, but Jabu jerked them away. "This is mine!" she screamed. "Get your thieving hands off." Mama and Uncle Njabulo were both yelling, and Solly stood by, looking as helpless as I felt.

Then I remembered the whistle that had been hanging around my neck for months. I had never used it. I pulled it out of my shirt and blew as hard as I could again and again. Jabu and the man by the bakkie turned to look at me. Mama and Uncle Njabulo stopped yelling at each other. Solly's mouth fell open. I didn't stop blowing until I felt a hand on my shoulder.

"That's enough, dear," said a quiet voice. I looked up into the calm face of Pastor Oscar. He smelled of the same soap Baba used to use. A small, thin man with the blue armband of the street committee stood beside him. A little boy hung behind—one I was sure I had seen racing away a few moments before.

"What is the meaning of this?" the man in the armband said as he strode toward Mama and Uncle Njabulo. My shoulders relaxed.

"My brother is recently late," Uncle Njabulo explained to the man from the street committee. His voice was calm, but his eyes shot fire. "His possessions belong to his family, and I have come to take them home."

"*We* are his family!" Mama's voice was a tight, hysterical squeal. She snatched the satin throw pillow off the pile of bedding Uncle held and clutched it to her chest. Her whole body trembled with anger.

"Do you have any proof of who you are?" the street committeeman asked Uncle. "Any documentation?"

Uncle Njabulo set down the stack of bedding and reached for his wallet.

Mama turned on the committeeman. "I don't question that he is my husband's brother," she said, "but that does not give him the right to walk into our house and rob us of everything we own! This is a disgraceful way to treat his own flesh and blood." She stretched her arms toward Solly, Jabu, and me.

Uncle pulled out his ID book and showed the committeeman. "I have here a certified copy of the Certificate of Death."

"I can't believe you are listening to him," Mama screeched. "The law doesn't allow this any longer. There has been no meeting of the elders! We've barely had time to mourn! And if you think I'm going to follow his traditions and be a second wife to this … this …" I could think of a few words I would have liked to use, but they weren't respectful.

The committeeman scrutinized the documents.

"Perhaps I can be of assistance." Pastor Oscar stepped around me. He reached into his suit coat and drew out a folded paper. "Brother Everest left a will."

"A will?"

"Yes." Pastor Oscar unfolded the paper. "I witnessed it for him a little more than a week ago. When the boy called me, I thought it might be needed. Brother Everest left his house and goods to his wife and children."

The thumping of my heart began to slow.

"That's impossible!" Uncle Njabulo said. "He didn't know he was going to die. Why would he make a will?"

Pastor Oscar looked at him. "Many people make a will when they are perfectly healthy. No one knows when God will call him home. You yourself, sir, should be prepared at any time to meet your Maker."

"Are you threatening me?" Uncle Njabulo took a menacing step toward Pastor Oscar. The little street committeeman stepped between them.

"Not at all," Pastor Oscar said calmly. "I am only stating a fact. One never knows what the future will bring. The Bible says, 'It is appointed unto men once to die and after that the judgment.' "

"Mr. Khumalo, wait," said the committeeman. "If your late brother made a will, then it must stand. Let me see it."

He took the paper from Pastor Oscar and studied it carefully. We waited in silence.

"This appears to be in order," he said at last. I found that I had been holding my breath and let it out slowly. He handed the paper back to Pastor Oscar and turned to Uncle Njabulo. "If you wish to bring a case and overturn the will, it must be done in a court of law. In the meantime you cannot take these things." He gestured at the back of the bakkie.

"Hey! Leave that alone!" Jabu darted after a boy making off with a pair of jeans. She bumped straight into Makatso. Makatso stepped back as though embarrassed to be caught in our yard.

"Thabo, stop!" I yelled.

Mboti was the one standing at the gate who gripped Thabo by his arm and relieved him of the stolen jeans.

Thabo shrugged and laughed. "Worth a try," he said to James as the two of them slunk away into the crowd.

Mboti silently handed the jeans to Jabu. She snatched them and looked away.

The committeeman pointed to Mboti and Makatso. "You and you, help unload. The rest of you get out of here." The onlookers scattered out of the gate, and I wondered how many of our things had gone with them.

The committeeman made a note of the bakkie's license number in his little book. He looked at Uncle Njabulo. "I will be nearby," he said, then turned to me. "If you need anything, call me."

I nodded. The committeeman stepped out of the gate and closed it behind him. I could hear him scolding the onlookers and sending them away. Uncle Njabulo scowled at the closed gate and then at me. Despite the clear blue sky, a suffocating cloud pressed down on us. No one spoke.

Jabu was the first to move. She gave Makatso a wary look, slowly gathered a load of clothes and carried them into the house, making a wide circuit around Uncle Njabulo.

Solly climbed onto the back of the bakkie and passed Makatso an end table. Mboti tossed two sofa cushions aside and reached to help Solly with the television.

I was about to pick up the sofa cushions when Uncle Njabulo took two strides toward me. He grabbed the whistle around my neck and wrenched it off. The cord burned as it broke and slid across my skin.

"Aaii!" I put my hand to my neck.

I didn't recognize the Zulu swear words Uncle Njabulo used. The English ones made the blood rush to my head. I pinched my lips together to keep from saying something disrespectful to my father's brother. He slapped me anyway, and my cheek burned.

Solly jumped down from the bakkie and Mboti stepped toward us, but his arms were full of the television. Before they had time to do anything disrespectful, Pastor Oscar stepped between us.

"There's no call for that." His voice was calm but firm. After all, Pastor Oscar was Uncle Njabulo's elder.

Uncle Njabulo spat more ugly words, but he didn't touch me again. I backed away toward Solly and Mboti. Mama stood under the jacaranda tree with both hands over her mouth as if she, too, was trying to hold back disrespectful words. Her eyes were large with fear. Makatso looked mildly amused.

"Let me get you a chair, so you and your friend can relax while the young people unload," Pastor Oscar told Uncle.

Solly climbed back up on the bakkie and handed Mboti two kitchen chairs. Pastor Oscar positioned them in the shade of the jacaranda. Mama drew back to the front of the house.

"There now. Make yourselves comfortable," Pastor Oscar said. "I'm sure they will not be long."

But Uncle Njabulo did not sit down. He stood, arms crossed, and watched with a sullen expression. "This is taking too long," he muttered when I passed him with my third load. I had to wait while Solly and Mboti maneuvered the entertainment center through the door.

Makatso followed with the shelves. Jabu laid a hand on his arm. "When we've finished, we should talk," she said. "There are things I need to know."

He shrugged her off. "Can't you see I'm busy, woman?"

I carried my load of clothes to Mama and Baba's room and dumped them on the bed. Most of the boxes were missing from the corner and top of the wardrobe. The wardrobe was pulled out from the wall as if they had intended to take it, but they had evidently changed their minds. Whether it was too heavy or too bulky to fit in the bakkie, I didn't know.

"What a mess!" Jabu said from the kitchen as I came out. Our "guests" had obviously helped themselves to snacks. Empty cool-drink cans and tins of meat were strewn on the counter along with an open packet of cookies and a half-finished tin of condensed milk. Jabu shook her head in disgust.

I clutched my arms across my chest. It was almost like being naked to think that those men—I didn't even want to call them relatives anymore—those men had been in our house when we weren't here, taking what they wanted and doing as they pleased. If they could do it once, what would keep them from coming back? I shivered.

Jabu put her arm around me. "Come on. Let's finish unloading so they can go."

Solly and Mboti were still fitting the entertainment center into place along the wall of the lounge when we passed through.

"More to the left," Mama said. "You have to leave room for the lamp over there."

Uncle Njabulo was no longer standing at the bottom of the steps. He and his friend were in the back of the bakkie. The mattresses from my bed and Jabu's lay half in the flowerbed where they had been tossed. The loveseat from our lounge teetered on the side wall of the bakkie a moment before Uncle Njabulo tipped it into the yard with the sickening crunch of splintering wood. Makatso jumped out of the way but did nothing to stop them.

"Wait!" Pastor Oscar called. "Let the young people help you."

The other man from KwaZulu shoved a box off the back of the bakkie and followed it quickly with another and another. Boxes tumbled after one another, bashing corners and rolling upside down.

Solly pushed past me. The words he was muttering were worthy of Uncle Njabulo, but before he reached it, the bakkie was empty. Uncle jumped down and headed for the driver's seat. He threw us an angry look, and I was glad I couldn't hear the words that came through his clenched teeth. The other man swung open the gate, and Uncle Njabulo drove out. He scraped the side of his vehicle on the fender of our car as he squeezed through, bumping along the sidewalk and over the curb. We heard the screech of tires as they took off up the street.

We stood a long time, staring at the open gate, afraid to move, afraid to breathe, afraid they would come back.

Makatso looked around with a snide smile. "I guess the bakkie is unloaded." He edged toward the gate. "So I'll be going." Even Jabu said nothing as he disappeared around the corner. Mboti picked up a box and started toward the house.

Chapter 18

Jabu thrust a broom into my hands. "Solly and Mboti are bringing in the beds. Better use this first."

I took it. I had avoided our room since we got back. I didn't want to see it raped by my uncle, but I couldn't put it off forever. The beds were gone. They were smaller and easier to transport than the one in our parents' room. But the wardrobe was heavy. Its doors stood open, revealing only the yellowed label glued to the back. The bookcase stood next to the door. Uncle Njabulo had no use for that, but our schoolbooks were missing from the shelves. He could sell them, no doubt. I didn't remember seeing them when we unloaded the bakkie. Perhaps they were in the cab on their way to KwaZulu after all.

My skating trophies and medals lay in a heap in the corner. I laid down the broom and knelt beside them. The leg had broken off the little lady doing a spiral at the top of my Gauteng Intermediate First Place trophy. I searched frantically through the pile until I found it and fitted the leg to her body. Perhaps with glue I might be able to fix it. The entire golden statuette was broken off another trophy. I clutched the little skater to my chest and bit my lip very hard. I didn't have time to cry. There was so much to clean up. These were only pieces of metal and plastic, memories of things past. I should be grateful that I still had a bed and clothes to put on in the morning, and that Uncle Njabulo hadn't claimed the house along with everything else. What if Baba hadn't made that will? I gathered the trophies and medals carefully and hid them at the bottom of the wardrobe.

Voices spoke in the hall, and I hurriedly brushed the tears from my cheeks.

"Careful!" Solly said. "You almost hit the light." Solly and Mboti maneuvered a bed frame into the room. I quickly swept aside my pile of dirt and huddled in the corner to give them space. Over their heads Michelle Kwan smiled down on us, but she had no body. The other half of the poster hung torn. It tickled Solly's neck. He reached up and pulled it out of the way.

Michelle Kwan's torn body fluttered to the floor while the boys tramped out. I ripped down the rest of the poster and crumpled it into a ball. Then I pulled the other skaters off the wall, tore them in tiny pieces, and buried them in the overflowing dustbin in the kitchen.

*   *   *

Jabu made sandwiches a little before seven. "Take these to Mama," she said, handing me a plate, "and make sure she takes her … vitamins," she finished lamely. I carried the plate into the bedroom with a cup of tea.

Mama looked up with red eyes from a pile of Baba's clothes on her bed. "Thank you, Sindi," she said as if I had brought her a dozen roses or a priceless gift.

"Don't forget …"

Mama looked at me, waiting.

"Don't forget your vitamins."

"My vitamins?" She furrowed her brow. "Oh, yes. Yes, of course." She fumbled for the bottle in her handbag and spilled the large pills into her hand. Her phone rang as I was leaving. She looked at the number and turned it off without answering.

I took Solly and Mboti each a sandwich and a can of Coke and the rest of the package of cookies. They sat on the pile of bricks by the back wall.

Mboti ran his hand over the top course. "Nice work. I've done a bit of building at my mother's. I could help you finish if you like. Things aren't too busy right now." He didn't mention losing his job. "I've been helping out at church, but I'm sure Pastor Oscar wouldn't mind."

Solly shrugged. "Maybe." He looked away. I didn't think he liked to think about the new room.

After he had eaten, Mboti left. He came inside "to say goodbye to your mother," he told us, but I think it was Jabu he really wanted to see.

"Goodbye," she said without turning from what she was doing.

"Goodbye, Mboti," I said, trying to make up for her rudeness. "Thank you for helping."

* * *

It was ten o'clock before I fell into bed exhausted, but it was hard to sleep. The skin on my neck burned where Uncle had pulled the whistle cord across it. Jabu turned the lock on our bedroom door without my asking, but I was still afraid to take my eyes off it for fear he would barge through and rip the covers off me to take to his family in the countryside. All night long I kept waking to see his scowling face looming over me, but it was only the moonlight on the lamp above my bed.

At five a.m. I was awake. Early morning skating was a habit hard to break. The streetlights had just gone out when I slid from under the sheet and slipped into my clothes. I headed to the kitchen for a cup of tea. Through the lounge door I glimpsed Solly, curled asleep on the love seat pushed against the front door with its splintered lock. Two bricks held up the broken frame.

Mama sat at the kitchen table with pieces of broken china in front of her.

"Are you taking me to the rink today?" I asked from the doorway.

Mama didn't answer. I tiptoed around a cardboard box that stood open in the middle of the floor, its side smashed in from falling off the bakkie. Bits and pieces of our life Before cluttered the counter. I filled the electric kettle and turned it on.

"What's that?" I asked while I waited for the water to boil. Mama opened and closed her mouth a few times, but no words came out.

I picked up a large curved piece of china and recognized the blue pattern of the vase that used to stand on our coffee table in Kempton. Mama kept it full of fresh flowers and yelled at anyone who came near it as if she thought we wouldn't be careful enough. She had never taken it out of its box once we moved here—afraid it would get broken in our crowded lounge, I guess. But even the box wasn't safe.

Mama fitted two of the large pieces together. There were so many tiny bits—how could she ever fix it?

The kettle whistled. I made two mugs of tea with lots of milk and sugar as my mother and I both liked it and sat at the table. I pushed a mug toward her. I wanted desperately to make things better for her.

"It was a wedding present," she said of the broken vase. "From my madam." I grew quiet. Mama never talked about her days as a domestic servant before she married my father.

"You don't remember them," she went on. "They emigrated before you were born. She sent you a lovely pink shawl from Canada." Mama put down one piece of blue china and picked up another to try against the one still in her hand. "Those were the days of apartheid, of course, before Africans like us were allowed to vote or even to live in Kempton Park."

I sipped my tea carefully.

Mama stared at the pieces of broken china in her hands as if in a dream. "My madam wasn't like the other white women I knew. She believed in me. She encouraged me to get an education, even paid for my textbooks. She was there when I received my diploma."

Mama picked up a curved triangular bit of china and stared at her image in what had been the glazed white inside.

"She was there at my wedding," she said in a voice so small I could hardly hear it. Suddenly her face contorted, and the tears came. "I married your father to get away from all this," she sobbed. "He had an education. We were going to give our children a chance—a chance for the life my madam believed we could have."

With one sweep of her arm the remains of the vase crashed to the floor along with her untouched mug of tea. Scalding liquid splashed my leg. A blue patterned shard landed in my lap. It nicked my palm as I clutched to keep it from falling to the floor with the rest.

"It was supposed to be different!" she wailed and buried her face in her arms.

Her pain seared my heart as the piece of broken porcelain stung my palm. After a few minutes I slid the bit of vase into the pocket of my pajamas and stood up to get the broom by the back door.

I dumped the shattered pieces of china into the dustbin and swept up the small bits and particles of glazed dust. Nothing remained but the one piece I had caught in my lap. Mama didn't lift her head when I took it with me to my room. I didn't feel much like skating today anyway.

* * *

I went back to school that week. Everyone knew my father had died and that's why I'd been away. But they didn't know what he died of—we just said pneumonia. James gave me a knowing look. I made sure to stay far away from him and Thabo at break time.

I didn't do very well in my exams. Uncle Njabulo had taken our textbooks, so there was nothing but my notes to revise even if I had had the energy, which I didn't. I sat at my desk and wrote an essay on economic opportunity in new South Africa for the civics exam, but all I could see was Takalani's empty desk and heaps of broken blue and white vases.

Chapter 19

Pastor Oscar sent a locksmith.

"No, ma'am," he explained with a grin when Mama asked how much we owed. "There's no charge. This is Kingdom work. I'll bring you a new deadbolt tomorrow. You can pay me for that." He winked at me and nodded politely as he left. "See you in church."

So on Sunday we went. We hadn't been anywhere since we moved except the little Baptist church in KwaZulu.

Mama made Solly put on one of Baba's business suits. I knew Zulus weren't supposed to wear a dead person's clothes until after the cleansing rituals, but Mama was so angry with Uncle Njabulo that she didn't care two cents about Zulu customs.

The jacket made Solly's shoulders look broad and grown up. The trousers were only a little short. But when Mama saw him, she cried, so Solly went back in the bathroom and changed into his school trousers and hung the suit in the wardrobe.

I had never been inside Wonderful Words of Life Church before. It smelled cool and musty as if the damp of rainy season never quite dried out. Inside was just a big room with a platform at one end. The motto from the sign was painted in fancy letters in an arc across the front wall: I HAVE COME THAT YOU MIGHT HAVE LIFE AND HAVE IT MORE ABUNDANTLY.

The service wasn't anything like our old church in Kempton Park. We sat on plastic chairs instead of pews and, instead of sitting or standing and singing politely, people yelled and waved their arms in the air. If I hadn't been missing my father so badly, I would probably have thought it was fun. A line of children in the front row did steps to the music like the traditional dances we learned last year for the Heritage Day program. A toddler looked up from nursing at his mother's breast and clapped his hands. My American friends would probably have been shocked.

Beside me Solly swayed to the beat. I hadn't seen him smile like that since the night of the ice show. Even Mama relaxed, and her face lost its worried frown.

Some of the ladies were having as much fun as the children. One woman in a pretty yellow turban closed her eyes and raised her arms in the air. She shouted, "Thank you, Jesus!" and her voice made me want to shout "thank you" too.

I almost didn't recognize Mboti when he stood to make the announcements. He wore a faded tweed sports jacket much too hot for the summer weather. I looked around nervously for his mother, but she didn't seem to be there.

"I'd like to remind you that the HIV support group meets on Thursdays." Mboti looked straight at where we sat in the second-to-the-back row. "You are welcome to come along even if you are just looking for information. We encourage everyone to be tested."

No one seemed surprised or embarrassed by the announcement. I wished Mama would go to the meeting. Now that she was on medications, I suspected it wasn't HIV eating her from the inside as much as the secret she was trying to carry alone.

At last Pastor Oscar got up to speak. "Turn with me in your Bibles to the book of Habakkuk, chapter three," he said in *isiZulu*.

Pages rustled around me. I was surprised at how many people had brought Bibles along. The nursing mother moved the toddler and started flipping through hers. We had an English Bible somewhere—maybe in one of the boxes from the old house—but I wasn't sure I had ever seen a Zulu Bible.

"Habakkuk was one of the prophets," Pastor Oscar explained. "You'll find him near the end of the Old Testament between the books of Nahum and Zephaniah." I'd never heard of Nahum or Zephaniah either, but that didn't seem to bother anyone else.

Pastor Oscar cleared his throat and began to read with feeling. "Though the fig tree does not bud and there are no grapes on the vines, though the olive crop fails and the fields produce no food, though there are no sheep in the pen and no cattle in the stalls …"

It sounded almost like poetry as he read, but what a sad poem. I looked at the congregation again. How many of these people came from the informal settlement at the end of the street? You couldn't always tell by looking. Even though the shacks had no plumbing, those people had pride too. Most of them got water to wash from the houses around or from the communal tap and dressed as well as they could. But how many of these people had jobs? How many had eaten breakfast this morning?

How many had HIV?

"Yet will I rejoice in the Lord," Pastor Oscar shouted. "I will be joyful in God my Savior!"

Rejoice? With no food and no crops, how could anyone rejoice? But the singing earlier …

The lady in the yellow turban closed her eyes and turned her face to the ceiling. She glowed with pleasure. The woman with the toddler leaned forward, her eyes fixed on the preacher.

Pastor Oscar had seemed soft-spoken when he came to our house, but get him behind the pulpit and he had a voice. He didn't need the sound system they were using, but they still had it turned up as loud as it could go.

Solly whispered in my ear, "We could have stayed home and listened to the sermon just as well." I giggled.

"The Sovereign Lord is my strength!"

Someone shouted, "Amen!" Another called out, "Thank you, Jesus!"

Jabu hunched her shoulders and looked at the floor as though she couldn't wait to get out of there. Mama sat beside me and cried into her handkerchief, but they were the good kind of tears—the kind that leave you feeling clean and ready for a new beginning.

"I will be joyful in God my Savior!" Pastor Oscar repeated.

The yellow-turban woman raised her arms over her head and shouted, "Hallelujah!"

"The Sovereign Lord is my strength!" Pastor Oscar said again, and pretty soon everyone was yelling "Praise God" or "Amen" or something else I didn't understand. It was almost as if they believed God was going to come down from heaven then and there and solve their problems. It didn't make sense to me.

Chapter 20

Monday was the first day of the summer holidays. I woke early—again. But I wasn't going to the rink today. The tattered corner of a skating poster was all that remained on the wall over my bed except a few grey wads of sticky tack.

"We don't have a lot of money right now," Mama had said after supper the night before. "I was thinking perhaps … we wouldn't go into Kempton every day for you to skate this summer. Once a week would be enough, don't you think?" Her eyes had begged me to agree and not to make this difficult for her.

I hadn't been on the ice since the show. My body longed to stretch and move. My soul longed to lose itself in the music and fly into the air like a bird. I wanted everything to be like it was Before. But Baba had paid the school fees for Bongiwe and the cousins before he died. Feeding all those people at the funeral had cost a lot, as did taking his body to KwaZulu. Skating wouldn't be the same without Baba. The weight in my chest would keep me tied to the ground, and I would fall like Sindi Skater, over and over. Besides, how could I face Nicola and Lerato without telling? So I agreed.

Now I rolled over and buried my face in the pillow. I had dreamed last night that I was gliding over the ice while beautiful music floated through me. It might have been one of the songs we sang in church. I couldn't quite remember. The lady in the yellow turban watched me, raising her hands and saying, "Thank you, Jesus."

"It was a dream. It was just a dream." I thumped up my pillow and lay down again.

Mama had left for work when I got up.

Jabu rummaged in her drawer. "Where is it? Sindi, have you seen my yellow knit top? The one with the gold threads through it?"

I thought. "No, not since …" Then we both remembered the day Uncle Njabulo had been there. Jabu swore. She pulled out the lacy white blouse instead.

"I'm going to the mall to look for a job," she announced as she put on her best earrings. She slipped on high-heeled shoes and examined herself in the mirror. She looked classy enough to work in that fancy dress shop across from Checkers. I almost asked if I could go with her before I remembered that even if Nicola and Lerato weren't at the rink at this hour, Andile would be in the little booth taking money and MakaMboti would be in the kiosk or handing out rental skates.

There was nothing to do at home after Jabu left. I tried stretching exercises and practice jumps in the back yard, but the half-finished walls of Solly's room brought a lump to my throat and made it hard to focus. I was springing for a double Axel when I saw Solly standing in the doorway, sipping a Coke. I landed on my right foot, stretched my arms for balance and gave a couple hops. Tackies on dirt don't glide like blades on ice.

"What are you doing?" Solly asked.

I sighed and dropped onto the step beside him. "Off-ice training." He didn't respond right away, and I could see he was trying to think of something to say.

"*Hawu, bantu.* I'm sorry." He seemed to regret my not being able to skate almost as much as I did.

Solly took his inline skates to Kempton Park to meet his friends from our old neighborhood at the church parking lot where they had built ramps and practiced tricks.

"What are you doing back so early?" I asked when he returned at lunchtime.

He shrugged and wouldn't meet my eye. He dumped his skates in the box in our room and went into the back yard where I saw him throwing broken bricks at the half-built foundations when he didn't know I was looking.

Jabu didn't get home until late. She hadn't found a job at a nice boutique in the mall as I knew she wanted. "Tomorrow I'll try the shops on Pretoria Road," she said.

Jammed with thin foam mattresses, mobile phones, and cheap dresses made in China, the Pretoria Road shops weren't exactly what she had hoped for, but Jabu went out every day that week. Every day she came home more discouraged.

Solly was out a lot too. Sometimes he took his skates; sometimes he didn't. When he was home, he sat on the pile of bricks in the back yard, smoking cigarette after cigarette, or he hung out on the corner with Makatso and Makatso's admirers. I wished he wouldn't.

Chapter 21

The week before Christmas Mama laid some money on the kitchen table. "Jabu, why don't you take Sindi Christmas shopping today."

It wasn't very much. Not like what she gave us for Christmas shopping last year. I looked at Jabu. I had figured we weren't going to have Christmas this year. Usually by the time school holidays came we were busy shopping, wrapping, and making decorations, teasing and trying to keep secrets. But this year ... I didn't feel much like celebrating anyway.

Mama's voice held a forced cheer as she stood at the sink and swallowed her "vitamins." "You can go into Kempton Park to the mall there. Make a day of it."

"You come too, Mama," I said.

She shook her head. "I'm too tired."

When she had gone to her room and closed the door, Jabu and I took a taxi to Kempton Park. "Know your status; get tested," said the poster at the taxi rank. I'd seen it before although I preferred to pretend that I didn't. I thought about Makatso.

"Jabu," I began as we crossed the mall parking lot. "Have you ..." She looked at me curiously. "Have you ever thought about getting tested?"

"Sindi!" she exploded. "How can you suggest such a thing?"

"I just thought ..." I stepped back from her anger. "I just thought maybe that was what you wanted to talk to Makatso about." I thought of saying "Mboti says everyone should be tested," but I didn't think Jabu wanted to know what Mboti had to say. "You can't take care of yourself if you don't know."

Jabu strode straight ahead. "Of all things ..."

* * *

Checkers had the cheapest presents. It reminded me of the Target store Jenni had taken me to in Lake Placid. We bought

Solly a CD he wanted that would be from both of us. Across
from the CDs was the aisle with the shaving lotions. I picked up
the red box that Baba's favorite came in and sniffed, but all I
could smell was cardboard. Jabu put it back on the shelf and
pulled me away.

She chose a scarf for Mama that was all silky and golden.
I had been looking at a black-and-white zebra-striped scarf, but
after I saw Jabu's that shimmered like sunshine, black and white
didn't look as pretty anymore.

"What about a picture frame?" Jabu suggested, but a
picture that didn't have Baba in it wouldn't feel right.

Jabu grew impatient. "Look, I still need to find something
for you. And I don't want you around when I do." She didn't
seem to be angry anymore, but she nudged me playfully. "How
about if we meet in half an hour at Woolies?"

I agreed. When Jabu was gone, I wandered up and down
the aisles. Mama didn't need electrical supplies or tools to fix the
car. I ended up in the row with the china dinner sets. There was a
blue-and-white set of dishes with a pattern of willow trees and
little Chinese houses and people on a bridge. I stared. It was the
same pattern as the one on the vase that got broken when Uncle
Njabulo threw the boxes off the back of his bakkie. There were
dinner plates and salad plates, cups and bowls. There were
serving bowls and salt sellers, and even a fancy cake server with a
blue-and-white china handle.

At last I found what I was looking for—a vase. It was
much smaller than the one that got broken. It would only hold a
single rose, or at most, two or three, and not a whole bouquet like
the ones Mama used to put on the coffee table in our old house
in Kempton Park. I weighed the vase in my hand. It was heavier
porcelain; not the delicate, thin stuff that had broken.

"But that means it won't break so easily," I told myself.
"Besides, a smaller house needs a smaller vase."

I looked at the price. I set the vase on the shelf and
counted my money. If I bought it, I wouldn't have enough left
for Jabu's present. I squeezed my eyes shut and remembered
Mama's face the morning when she tried to put together the

pieces of the broken vase. I remembered the pain, and I wanted more than anything to fix it for her. This vase wasn't as big as the old one; it wasn't as elegant. But I wanted her to look at it and to remember that someone believed in her. Me.

I picked up the vase and walked straight to the checkout counter before I could change my mind.

* * *

When I came out of Checkers, I turned left. I thought I might still have enough for a pair of earrings for Jabu from the little shop with the sparkly necklaces near the ice rink.

My steps slowed as I neared the rink. It was the middle of the day—public session. The figure skaters wouldn't be here. It was too crowded to jump or spin at a public session during the school holidays.

I stood at the rail in front of the big windows and watched the skaters. The sound of the music drifted through the glass, and my whole body strained to stroke in time with it. Right. Left. Body straight. The crowd of skaters inside went round and round. I was five years old when Solly and I had stood here watching for the first time.

"That's what I'm going to do," Solly had announced. He pointed to a big boy with long, straight black hair sticking out of his knit cap. The boy leaned over so far when he came around the corners that he trailed his fingers on the ice.

"Me too." It was not the school holidays then, and the ice was not crowded. Mariki had glided in flowing dance patterns up one side of the oval and down the other. Even then she was good. I didn't know her name that day; I didn't know how stuck up she was. I only knew that she skated like a bird, skimming over water, and I wanted to fly as well. I couldn't take my eyes off her. I wouldn't leave until Mama went into the rink and signed me up for lessons.

Lessons. What would Liselle say when she found out I hadn't skated during the holidays? Mama had said once a week, but she hadn't meant it. I hadn't been one single time.

I backed away from the glass and pushed through the Christmas shoppers. Maybe I would never know what Liselle would say. There wouldn't be any more money when school started than there was now. Or maybe Sindi Skater would have shrunk so small that I wouldn't be able to find her. I wouldn't remember how to fly like a bird, and Liselle would be angry with me and yell as Nicola's mother did when Mariki didn't skate the way she wanted. And I would never get to go back to Lake Placid. Ms. Etherington wanted someone who worked hard. I tried to swallow the lump in my throat. I wasn't worth investing in.

The mall was crowded with shoppers. Colored lights framed the window displays, and Christmas music played on the sound system—music that made me want to skim over the ice, music that made me angry that I couldn't.

I was so deep in my own thoughts that I almost walked into Lerato and Nicola. They were just ahead inside Woolworths department store—Woolies. Lerato held up an orange knit top and struck a model's pose. Nicola nodded enthusiastically and grabbed a similar pink one from the rack.

Part of me wanted to rush over and hug them and say how much I had missed them. The other part of me knew I couldn't—not without explaining why I hadn't been at the ice rink in three weeks. Not without awkward questions that might let out the secret.

I stopped in the middle of the mall corridor so suddenly that a woman bumped into me from behind and stepped on my heel. She scolded. Other shoppers flowed around me. I dodged between the people to the far side of the corridor. Beyond Woolies' plate glass windows Lerato and Nicola laughed and talked as they picked other items and headed for the changing rooms. I stayed outside, alone in the mass of holiday shoppers.

The river of people swept me along until I came to the little shop with the sparkly necklaces in the window. Fake snow decorated the corners as though this were Europe or North America instead of Africa where Christmas was the hottest time of year.

The earrings in the window cost more than I had. "Don't you have any less expensive ones?" I asked the girl at the counter. She pointed to a rack along the back wall. Even there I had to search before I found any that I could afford.

I was just coming out of the shop when I saw Nicola's mother. Her arms were full of shopping parcels, and she had her phone to her ear. I stepped behind a rack of beaded handbags by the door and willed her to pass without seeing me. But she clicked her phone shut and waved.

I couldn't believe it. Now what was I going to do? *Smile for the judges, Sindi.* I stretched my lips and showed some teeth, but somehow I didn't think it sparkled. *Relax, Sindi! You can do this!*

I stepped from behind the beaded handbags and breathed deeply. *You went to KwaZulu-Natal to visit your father's family. That's not even a lie. You can't wait to get back on the ice.* Oh, how true that was! I couldn't have pretended to Liselle, but I could pretend to Nicola's mother.

Just as I raised my hand to wave, Nicola emerged from the crowd and greeted her mother. When I glanced left, I made out Lerato's head bobbing away among the shoppers. Mrs. Brodowski bent over the Woolies bag as Nicola showed her what she had bought. She hadn't been waving to me. She had waved at Nicola. I stepped back behind the handbag display and ducked to study the price tag on an elegant black and gold one. Hopefully, they wouldn't come in here.

But Nicola pointed and came straight toward me. I slid down a side aisle, wishing I could make myself invisible. Nicola stopped outside the shop and pointed to a beaded necklace in the display window. I let out my breath slowly. She hadn't seen me either. I held perfectly still in the back of the shop until they moved down the corridor.

I crept back to the door and watched until they went into another shop. Jabu stood in front of Woolies, checking her watch and looking impatiently up and down the crowded corridor. I darted out of my hiding place and grabbed her arm.

"Come on. Let's go home." I strode toward the exit without looking back.

Chapter 22

A man stood at our gate when we arrived home. He was taller than Pastor Oscar and not as wide. His clothes were well-pressed and professional-looking, but not fancy.

"May I help you with something?" Jabu asked.

"Leah Khumalo lives here?"

Jabu nodded. "She's our mother."

I twisted my neck to better see the formal-looking papers in the man's hand. "In the high court of Northern Gauteng Province," they began. My eyes opened wide. I scanned down the page. My mother's name was there. So was Uncle Njabulo's. The man's head swiveled on his neck to stare at me. I took a step back, and he drew the papers to his chest. "I must speak with your mother."

Jabu unlocked the gate and motioned for the man to come in. "I'll call her," she said and jogged up the steps into the house. The man followed more slowly. I slid through the gate and leaned against the post. Waiting. Watching. My stomach in my throat.

"I am Leah Khumalo," Mama said when she came to the door. "How may I help you?"

"Notice of Motion," the man said crisply. "Sign here." He handed her a clipboard. Mama's hand trembled only a little as she took it and signed. "If you intend to oppose this Application, you must notify the Applicant's attorneys in writing and file your Opposing Affidavits, if any, within two weeks of notification." Mama blinked several times as she handed back the clipboard. I don't think she understood what he was talking about any more than I did.

The man nodded as he took the clipboard. "Thank you. Have a nice day."

He turned and walked swiftly back down the steps toward me. I stumbled backward to get out of his way, but he never looked at me as he went out and started down the street in the direction of the Community Chat. He crossed the street before he reached it, and I wondered if he had no more desire to confront Makatso's *tsotsis* than I did.

"Gangsters, that's what they are," I murmured, watching James and Thabo.

I closed the gate and locked it carefully. By the time I got inside Mama had retreated to her room. I thought she would cry, but if she did, I didn't hear her. Her face was hard and her voice like ice when she came out.

"Your uncle is challenging the will," she said. "He wants the house along with everything else. The court date is after Christmas. We will all go. That judge will have to look Everest's children in the eye before he makes a decision."

* * *

I wrapped my presents carefully in pretty paper that Jabu had bought. I had forgotten to leave money for that. I pushed aside the clothes to hide them in the bottom of the wardrobe. My skates were there, where I had hidden them weeks ago. I pulled a fleece over them so I wouldn't have to see and buried the presents in the fleece.

Sindi Skater pushed against the walls I used to lock her in. She wanted out. Seeing the rink, hearing the music, had cracked the door so I could hear her whispered calls for freedom. While Jabu looked for a job and Solly hung out at the corner, I jogged. I skipped rope. I stretched. I sat on empty space with my back pressed against the wall until my muscles screamed so loudly I thought the neighbors would hear them over the radio next door.

And I jumped. I bent my knees and sprang into the air, pulling my arms tightly to my chest. I imagined I was doing loop jumps, Salchows, flips, and Axels and did them over and over as I would do on the ice until my whole body ached.

* * *

The Friday before Christmas was hot and still. I was bored. I clicked on the television in the lounge and sank onto the loveseat, careful not to kick the bricks that held up its broken frame. A vision in pale blue floated across the screen, her free leg arched gracefully over her head. She turned and spiraled backward over the ice.

Sindi Skater swelled inside me and swept my breath away. I leaned forward, my body aching to stretch and glide.

I recognized the girl and her music. She trained at Lake Placid. She had smiled at me once, but we never shared the ice. She was a senior skater; I was only intermediate. *This must be a rebroadcast of last year's Worlds.*

I glanced out the window. It was late afternoon. A thunderstorm was brewing in the west over the city. No one would be home for a while yet. Mama was at work; Jabu was looking for a job. Solly would come when he got hungry. No one would know if I watched just a little.

I sat on the edge of the seat, leaning forward. My finger hovered over the power button, ready to press at the first sign of anyone coming.

"Exquisite!" the commentator remarked. "This is Suzanna's first World Competition. She doesn't have a chance to medal this year, but she is definitely one to watch for the next Olympics."

That was what I had hoped they would say of me someday. I clutched my stomach with both arms and blinked moisture from my eyes, but I couldn't tear them from the screen. The girl finished her program and waved to the cameras when her scores were announced. Her smile shone with all the dreams that had been mine.

They announced the next skater. Her music was louder and bouncier. I turned the volume low and glanced out the window. Still no one.

I wiped my nose on the sleeve of my T-shirt. *My sit spin is lower than hers.* She wobbled on her triple Lutz and left off the second jump of the pass. *It's not fair!* I wanted to scream. But I didn't. I bit my lip and watched the skating through the blur of my tears.

"I don't trust him, Solly," came Jabu's strident voice. I turned and looked through the window in time to see her pushing open the gate. Solly came after her, slouching and shuffling his feet.

"Watch it!" Solly said when she nearly swung the gate shut on top of him.

I dropped the remote in my hurry to turn off the television and fumbled for it under the coffee table.

"It's none of your business who I hang out with," Solly whined as they crossed the yard. "Just because you don't want to go out with him ..."

I found the remote and clicked the TV off as they reached the door. They would have caught me if they hadn't stopped to argue. I left the remote on the table and slipped quietly from the room.

"Why can't you leave me alone?" Solly complained. "You're not my mother."

I closed the bedroom door and leaned against it as they entered the lounge. My pulse throbbed in my neck. My heart beat against my ribs. Why was I so afraid I would be caught? It wasn't like there was anything wrong with watching skating. I had seen these same Worlds live when they happened. But that was Before. Now was different. I didn't want them to see my chest torn open and my beating heart ripped out.

Jabu and Solly were still arguing. "Go on," Solly said. "I want to watch the rugby game."

"But you always—" Jabu stopped abruptly.

Solly must have turned on the TV. The skating would still be there. That last skater—the one who won the competition—would be skating her program to "Midsummer Night's Dream." I remembered how she had arched her back with impossible grace as she floated in a wide arc over the ice. I remembered how the audience had stood to cheer when she finished that final breathtaking spin.

Jabu and Solly were arguing again. This time I couldn't hear the words—only the low, intense murmur of their voices. Solly's voice rose defiantly. "Why shouldn't she—?"

"Hush!" Jabu said, and Solly was quiet.

I crawled onto my bed and pulled a blanket over my head. My father wasn't the only thing I had lost. I missed the freedom of vaulting into the air like a bird, the power of a tight spin, the joy of light steps over the ice. I missed Lerato and Nicola, Kobus, and even Mariki a little bit.

Someone knocked lightly on the door. I didn't answer. Solly slipped in and rummaged in his cardboard box for his inline skates. I heard him, but I kept my face to the wall and pretended to be asleep until he went out again. Now I knew why Mama stayed in her room with the curtains closed.

Chapter 23

I woke early on Christmas morning. If this were KwaZulu-Natal we would be getting up in the dawn to visit the graves between the cattle kraal and the garden. "To greet the ancestors," Uncle Njabulo would say. "Nonsense," Mama would whisper to us children. "We are only paying our respects like good Christians."

This year there would be new graves—Uncle Thulani's baby's and my father's. He was an ancestor now, and I wished I could throw my arms round him and greet him. Thanks to HIV, the baby would never be an ancestor.

I heard Mama moving in the kitchen. We hadn't planned to celebrate. After giving me the money to buy presents, Mama hadn't said another word about Christmas. Then yesterday she must have decided she was depriving her children, because she came home with armloads of groceries and sweets and Christmas crackers.

I hopped out of bed and greeted her, "Happy Christmas, Mama."

Mama smiled weakly. "Happy Christmas to you."

I stood at the table in my thin summer pajamas and helped her to chop pumpkin, marrows, and onions. She pulled a packaged chicken from the fridge and peeled off the plastic wrap.

"Chicken?" I asked. "But it's Christmas."

When I was little and Baba had a whole week for the holiday, we always went to KwaZulu-Natal. Baba and the uncles would slaughter a sheep. I felt more connection with my Zulu ancestors that one day than at any other time in the year. Once Mama started working in an office and only had Christmas Day off, KwaZulu-Natal had been too far. Lamb bought at the butcher's didn't taste the same.

"Why are we having chicken?" I asked.

"Because I don't—like—mutton." Her voice was tight and clipped like the knife she used to hack at the bones of the chicken. It wasn't even a real chicken with feathers on it. This was the kind of grocery-store chicken all the white people in Kempton Park would put on their braais today to grill with pork chops and boerewors and pieces of steak. It didn't feel very Zulu.

Solly stood in the kitchen door with his jeans still unzipped and his belt hanging unbuckled. "What's the chicken for?"

Mama exploded. "Will you stop going on at me about the chicken! A few things have changed around here in case you haven't noticed. Now you can eat it, or you can go without."

I stared at them. Solly didn't say anything disrespectful. He didn't say anything at all. He walked out and slammed the door. When I took the chicken wrappings to the bin on the back porch so they wouldn't stink in the house, I found him sitting on the pile of bricks with a cigarette.

"It's time for presents now," I said.

He startled as though he hadn't heard me come out. He flicked the ash from his cigarette. "I'll come in a minute."

* * *

Mama opened Jabu's scarf first.

"Lovely, Jabu. Thank you."

"I thought it would go with your cream suit."

Mama gave Jabu a peck on the lips. "You have such good taste." Her cheerfulness sounded forced.

Solly gave her a gold necklace.

"Oo, that's pretty," I said, but Mama looked at him as if she were wondering where he got the money.

"Open mine." I watched her eagerly. I didn't have a box. The shape of the vase was unmistakable under the paper. But it was the pattern I wanted her to see, the pattern that matched the broken vase from her old madam.

Mama untied the ribbon and pulled away the tissue. A puzzled look came over her face as she looked at the vase. I was sure that she recognized the pattern, but this seemed cheap and clunky compared to the delicate china that had meant so much to her. I felt foolish to have thought my gift would make her believe in herself again.

"Thank you, Sindi," Mama said and kissed me lightly on the mouth, but I don't think she understood what it was I had wanted to give her.

Mama gave us all practical presents, socks and underwear and things that we needed. Jabu gave me a pink knit top that looked a lot like the ones Lerato and Nicola had been trying on. Solly's present to me was in a little box. I wondered if it could be jewelry like the necklace he had given Mama, but the package didn't rattle. I pulled off the red and green paper and opened the lid. Inside was white tissue paper, crumpled tissue paper that had been used before. I pulled it back and found a hundred-rand note.

"I thought you might like to go skating sometime," Solly explained. My heart leapt like a bird rising. This was enough for several trips to the rink.

Mama lifted her necklace and eyed him. "Solly, where did you get this kind of money?"

Solly's eyes flared. "I didn't steal it if that's what you mean."

"I didn't say that," Mama said, but you could see it was what she was thinking. "I don't like you hanging out with those *tsotsis* on the corner. I don't think they're a good influence. I don't know what to think of you anymore."

Solly stood up so quickly that presents scattered.

"Where do you think you are going, young man? Come back here when I'm talking to you." But he walked out of the door without stopping.

Mama looked after him for a few moments and then began gathering up the torn wrapping paper and stuffing it into a used shopping packet to throw in the dust bin as if nothing had happened. "If we're going to church, we need to get dressed."

"I get the shower first." Jabu gathered her gifts and headed for the bathroom.

I gathered Solly's things along with my own and carried them to our room. The T-shirts in his box were a jumbled mess. I refolded them to make room for his presents. That was when I realized—there were no inline skates in the box, and Solly hadn't taken them with him when he stormed out. Slowly I laid the last T-shirt on the pile.

* * *

We went into Kempton Park for church. Solly didn't go. The service seemed dull and boring after Wonderful Words of Life. The sermon was short, but I still couldn't keep awake. This preacher didn't talk as loud as Pastor Oscar. He didn't seem to expect God to come down and act in our lives in the same way Pastor Oscar did.

We smiled and shook hands with people after the service, but no one asked any awkward questions. No one seemed to realize we hadn't been there in months. I wasn't sure they even remembered us. It wasn't like Wonderful Words of Life. Everyone was too eager to get home to their own Christmas celebration to think about being a community.

Chapter 24

The next morning I slowly stirred the milk and sugar in my teacup and considered going back to bed like Mama had. Jabu tore at a piece of bread. She didn't seem to have the energy to go out again looking for a job.

I scratched my head. The swirls and curves Jabu had woven before the ice show still covered my scalp, but fluff was growing out at the roots. Jabu lifted a handful of matted braids and beads. "We really should do your hair."

I shrugged.

Jabu frowned; then she smiled. She laid her spoon down and took a sip of tea while she studied my hair silently. "Yes. We'll do your hair this morning." I could almost see the little light bulb go on over her head like in cartoons.

"What are you thinking?" I asked.

"You'll see." She drained her cup and carried it to the sink. "Go get dressed."

"Why do I need to get dressed to sit at the kitchen table while you braid my hair?"

"Just do as I say. All right?"

When I came out of the bedroom in my jeans and a T-shirt, she was standing by the front door with the small folding table we used to use by the pool. "Bring a chair, Sindi."

"Where are we going?"

"Outside." Jabu marched through the gate onto the sidewalk.

"We're going to do my hair out here?"

"Is there anything wrong with that?" She set up the table in the shade of the wall and began arranging combs and picks and the little box that held my beads.

I looked up the street toward the church and then down to the Community Chat. For once Makatso wasn't holding court.

Jabu followed my glance toward the Community Chat and seemed relieved not to see him there. She patted the chair. "Now sit."

I sat.

The morning was still cool. A lot went on in Tembisa that we missed behind our closed gate. Taxis hooted, announcing they had space. Little children stuck their hands through the palisade of the crèche across the street and waved. I couldn't help smiling and waving back. No one had ever waved to me in our old neighborhood of Kempton Park. A young woman with a bright orange beach towel holding her baby on her back passed us and joined the line outside the church. Packets of mealie meal, beans, ground nuts and rice, and bottles of cooking oil peeked from the shopping bags of those who came out.

Jabu carefully undid each tiny braid. I loved the dreamy feeling of her fingers on my head. My mind drifted somewhere above the township, and if it weren't for the bouncy music from the radio next door, I might have fallen asleep. I closed my eyes. Behind my lids Sindi Skater danced across the ice to the music. She didn't make one mistake.

"Sindi!"

I startled awake. I had jerked my arms to my chest for a double-rotation jump.

"What were you thinking?" my sister asked in disgust.

"Sorry."

"Let's do something creative today," Jabu said, seeming to forget her annoyance.

"Like what?"

She took a strand in her hand without answering and began to braid.

She had only made a half dozen small braids when a little boy ran up to her. "Auntie wants to know how much you charge," he asked in *isiXhosa*. He pointed down the street to the sweets vendor, sitting under her striped umbrella outside the Community Chat.

"Tell her one hundred rand. More if she wants the braids very tiny," Jabu said.

I gasped. "I can't pay you a hundred rand," I protested.

Jabu swatted my shoulder. "You're my sister. You're also my advertising," she whispered when the boy had gone. "It's working."

I grinned.

The boy was back in a moment, sucking a sweet. "She says, when you are finished here, come and do hers."

Jabu nodded. "I'll come." The boy trotted off. "Maybe we'll do something simple after all." She began taking larger strands of hair to twist together with the small braids she had already made.

"But it had better look nice," I said. "Remember; I'm your advertising."

"Don't worry."

A neighbor came up from the taxi, balancing a huge sack of mealie meal on her head with two shopping bags in each hand. "I didn't know you braided hair," she said. "I haven't had time to do mine." It was hidden beneath a paisley scarf.

"I'm fully booked this morning," Jabu said, "but I could take you this afternoon."

"I'd like that. At two o'clock?" They agreed. The gate clicked behind her.

I thought Jabu would be happy, but suddenly she swore.

"Ooow!" I grabbed my scalp where she had nearly pulled the hair right out of my head. Pretty Mogane strutted up the street in a yellow knit top. When she passed the crèche on the far side of the street, gold threads glittered in the sunshine. "She's wearing your shirt."

"She certainly is." Jabu jerked my hair this way and that as she braided. "It was probably a Christmas present from her new boyfriend." She swore under her breath.

"Aren't you going to get it back?"

Jabu pulled one strand of hair across another. I winced and wished I hadn't asked. "How could I prove it was mine?"

I had to agree. Gradually the sound of her breathing returned to normal, but her hands never quite relaxed, and I knew she still seethed inside.

"Jabulile! Sindiswa!" Mboti's voice made me jump.

"Hi, Mboti." I held my head perfectly still and didn't look at him. Jabu grunted something, but I think she was still watching Pretty at the far end of the street in her gold-and-yellow top.

Mboti leaned against the wall and watched us. "I thought maybe I would see you in church yesterday."

Jabu didn't say anything.

"We went to Kempton Park," I said.

"Oh." Mboti sounded disappointed. "About that group we have on Thursday ..." he began again. "It's not just for people with HIV, you know. It's for anyone who wants information."

I held my breath. Jabu wanted to talk to Makatso, but Makatso was not the one to give her the information she needed.

"Information about testing, for example," Mboti said. "If you know your status, you can protect yourself and the people you love."

"We're fine," Jabu said. "We don't need your help." She snapped at him as if he were the one who had stolen her shirt and given it to her rival. I guess she wasn't thinking about going to that support group.

"I didn't mean ..."

"I said, 'we're fine'. "

Mboti was silent a moment.

"How are you doing, Sindi?" he asked at last. "My mother says you haven't been coming to the ice rink. She misses you. Everyone does. Liselle tried to call your mother's mobile, but all she got was the voice mail."

Sindi Skater stirred in my heel as if she might wake up and want to get out, but I ground my foot on the sidewalk and squashed her.

"Why don't you just leave us alone?" Jabu exploded. "No one asked for your help. No one wants you coming around, spying on us and then blabbing our business at the ice rink."

"I'm not spying on you."

But Jabu's voice rose. "I can just see you, spreading ugly stories to MakaLerato and that Brodowski woman."

Mboti took a step back, and Jabu pressed after him, all her anger at Makatso spewing onto Mboti. "You don't even have a real job, do you? You just hang out at the church because you don't have anything better to do. Or is it the free food?" She jerked my shoulders into position and seized a hank of hair. "It's surely not to pick up girls. They're all sick."

Mboti's eyes flashed. "Is that what you think? All right, I'll leave you alone. But for your information, the church is doing good work. We're a community. We help each other. We give and receive. You weren't above taking Pastor Oscar's help when your uncle was here. And what have you given in return—shut away behind your insulating walls?"

Mboti was as fired up as Jabu. "You've always thought you were too good for me, haven't you, Jabulile Khumalo, and where has it gotten you? Where? Have you even bothered to find out? There's a testing center at the hospital," he threw back as he whirled and stomped up the street toward the church.

Jabu didn't make a sound. She might have stopped breathing, but her fingers kept twisting my hair in tiny, tight braids, pulling like a drowning woman desperately holding on. At last she sniffed and stopped braiding to wipe her nose.

Chapter 25

Everyone slept in Sunday morning. Everyone except me. I slipped out and went to the church. I slid onto a bench in the back and watched. "Community," Mboti had said. Pastor Oscar talked about Jesus. Jesus was an important teacher, even God, some people said, but he wasn't afraid to touch lepers.

"Leprosy starts as a skin disease that deadens the nerves," Pastor Oscar explained. "Without pain the patient doesn't avoid injury and may lose hands or feet. Secondary infections absorb cartilage until the fingers and toes are twisted and deformed and the nose disappears." A woman near me grabbed hers as if to be sure it was still there.

Mboti sat in the front row. He had made his announcement again about the HIV support group. Now he sat with his head bowed, as though he was praying while the preacher talked.

"Leprosy is a foul and ugly disease," Pastor Oscar said. His voice was hard and strong. "People in those days were as afraid of leprosy as people today are of AIDS." He looked from one listener to another. "Their friends and loved ones rejected them. They feared to even touch them. They drove them from their homes. The law required lepers to call out 'unclean' if anyone came near."

Someone gasped.

"It must have been a lonely life." Pastor Oscar's face grew soft. "But Jesus touched the lepers! Jesus healed the lepers! Jesus made the unclean to be clean!" His voice rose to a shout.

Calls of "Hallelujah" and "Praise God!" rang out.

"Jesus took away the filth of sin not just on their skin or in their bones, but from their hearts!"

A woman began to sob. She rocked back and forth, clutching her arms to her chest. The woman next to her put an arm around her shoulders. Others were crying, too. Shouts of "Forgive me" and "Heal me" replaced the "Hallelujahs."

"Come to Jesus," Pastor Oscar cried. "Come to Jesus, and he will not turn you away."

People began to crowd down front, falling to their knees, shouting and crying. I huddled on my bench in the back corner, hardly daring to move. But I didn't leave. I couldn't. There was something here that I wanted.

* * *

"Mboti!" I called when the service had ended.

He was crossing the swept-earth churchyard toward the metal shipping container near the community garden. He stopped and turned. "Sindi! It's good to see you."

I trotted toward him. "I've been thinking about what you said the other day—about not helping anyone. You were right. We're too scared of someone finding out to get to know anyone in the neighborhood. We never help anyone. We just hide."

Mboti looked at the ground. "I … I was angry with your sister," he said. "I shouldn't have talked like that. I'm sorry."

"But it's true. And I don't want it to be. I want … I want to do something … like you."

His face broke into a broad grin. "I'm getting ready to go visit someone now. Wanna come? They have a new baby."

"A baby? I'll come." I hesitated. "It's not in the informal settlement, is it?"

Mboti shook his head. "No. It's not in the settlement."

He pulled a key from his pocket, unlocked a padlock, and swung open the wide door of the container.

"What *is* all this?" I asked.

One end of the shipping container was piled with forty-kilo gunnysacks of rice and mealies. Cases of soap and canned goods crowded shelves. Black trash bags spilled used clothes onto the floor.

"It's supplies we've collected from individuals or churches in Kempton Park. Some hypermarkets donate goods near their expiry date, and we get them to people who can use them. I could really use your help."

He started pulling things off shelves and stuffing them into a plastic shopping parcel—powdered soup, canned meat, a bag of beans, and a tin of powdered milk. "And this is for the baby." He handed me a packet of nappies and a soft green blanket. He threw a satchel over his shoulder and picked up a bag of garden vegetables. "Let's go."

The informal settlement was on our right as we walked. I found my hand wandering to the whistle I had replaced around my neck.

"You know, most of the people who live here are good people," Mboti said. "No different from you or me. All they want is a decent life for their families. But when they're crowded together like that … Well, some people forget what it means to live like a child of God." I knew he was thinking about James and the other boy. "They aren't all like that, Sindi."

"I know." My stomach felt like a lump of undigested porridge.

Mboti steered me down a side street that was more dirt than asphalt and up an alley nearly blocked by two old cars. The one in front didn't look as if it had moved in years. The back window was out and covered with plastic held in place by wide grey tape.

"*Molo*, Evelyn!" Mboti called.

A woman in a flowered headscarf rose from her plastic chair outside a cement-block house. Her round cheeks glowed, and she looked around as if to be sure the neighbors noticed that she had visitors. "*Molweni!*"

A girl peeked from the open doorway. She didn't look any older than Jabu.

"S'bo, look who's here," Evelyn called.

Mboti and Evelyn chatted for a while in isiXhosa, but I understood most of it—something about a woman across the courtyard who had died.

"I told her she needed to have her blood tested," Evelyn said. "She wanted the doctor to give her medicine to make her well, but she wouldn't get tested. Then this morning we heard the wailing." She shook her head. "So unnecessary. But come in, come in."

Evelyn led the way into the house. I looked back over my shoulder at the house in mourning. The woman died because she didn't get the right medicine. She didn't get the right medicine because she hadn't been tested. She refused to get tested because … because she was keeping a secret she was too afraid to tell. I shivered and followed Evelyn into the house.

* * *

The house was one room divided by a yellow cupboard and a striped curtain with a red fringe. A small refrigerator stood in one corner with a television on top of it. Odd bits of carpet and old linoleum covered the uneven cement floor. A crocheted doily and a brass urn decorated the little table. I would never complain about the size of our lounge again.

A tiny wail came from behind the curtain. Evelyn disappeared. S'bo took a tin from the cupboard and mixed milk powder with warm water, testing it on her arm.

"This is who Sindi has come to see," Mboti explained when Evelyn reappeared with the baby, bundled in the soft green blanket. His tiny eyes were squeezed shut. His little pink mouth opened. Evelyn held out the baby to me, and S'bo handed me the bottle. As soon as I popped it into his mouth the crying stopped.

"Are you having any trouble with the formula?" Mboti asked. "The nurse can come to see you on Thursday if you have any questions."

S'bo shook her head. "We're doing well. I'm taking my medicines and so is Mother. We remind each other."

I glanced from one to the other. They must both be HIV positive, but they talked so freely with Mboti. They weren't trying to keep a secret.

Mboti nodded. "Any nightmares?" Both women shook their heads. "You're lucky! When I started my meds—whew! I had the craziest dreams and woke up screaming." Mboti laughed. "But the side effects don't last long."

The baby sucked noisily in my arms.

S'bo touched his head. "In another month the baby can

be tested, but I took the medicine before he was born, so we're hoping he'll be all right."

Mboti nodded. "Let's pray." He took the girl's hand in his and laid the other on the baby in my arms. S'bo took her mother's hand and Evelyn took my arm. I had a feeling they had done this before. Mboti prayed. It wasn't a long prayer, but he asked God to take care of this little family, to keep them healthy, and to protect the baby.

"Amen," he said.

"Amen," said Evelyn and her daughter together.

I squeezed the baby and whispered "Amen," and I meant it with all my heart.

Chapter 26

It was dusk when Mboti left me at my front gate. Solly's laughter came from the group outside the Community Chat. The sounds of Tembisa filled the warm night—a distant radio, the grinding gears of a lorry, the murmur of voices. I wandered nearer and stood in the shadows between the streetlights. Solly leaned against the container as if he did this all the time. There were no girls tonight. Only young men and the boys like James and Thabo who wanted to be like them.

Makatso took a long drag on his cigarette. "I've slept with so many girls, I'm probably single-handedly responsible for the AIDS epidemic in Tembisa!"

James laughed. "You're bad, Makatso!"

"Have you been tested?" Solly's voice asked quietly when the laughter had died down.

Makatso laughed. "Why would I want to get tested? They'd just give me some lecture about being responsible and using condoms." His voice went low and he swayed in that sexy way of his. "I like the feel of skin on skin." The other boys laughed. Solly didn't. I was glad.

I stepped into the light. "You're a fool, Makatso."

He dropped his cigarette and stared as if he had seen a spirit.

"Have you ever visited the AIDS ward? Do you know what hopelessness looks like? What it smells like?"

"Sindi?" Solly crushed out his cigarette. "What are you doing here?"

"You gamble your life and the lives of everyone you touch."

Solly turned me around and marched me toward our gate before I had a chance to say more. I looked back over my shoulder at the boys under the streetlight. How many would be dead like Baba in a few years? James laughed nervously. Thabo looked away and wouldn't meet my gaze.

Solly swore. He smelled like stale tobacco.

"Don't listen to them, Solly! I don't want you to die." I didn't know when I had started crying.

He swore again and pushed me through our gate. The flicker of the television shone through the open door to the lounge while my brother steered me around the house to the back. I sniffed and wiped my nose on my sweaty arm.

The stack of bricks for the unfinished room loomed in the shadows along the back wall. One end had tipped and scattered bricks in the dust. Solly steered me around them to a place by the foundation trench where I could sit on bricks and lean against the half-built wall.

He squatted in front of me. "You're right," he said. "Makatso is a fool." He fished in his pocket for a tissue that still had a clean corner and gave it to me. I blew my nose.

He shifted some bricks and arranged a second seat. We sat silently and gazed into the trench. Rain had partially eroded it.

"I miss Baba," I whispered. Solly didn't say anything for a long while. At last he spoke.

"I quarreled with Baba the night of your ice show." The darkness hid his face in shadow. "We were sitting in the car, waiting for you to come out." His voice trembled, but he didn't stop. "He tried to tell me how he had betrayed our mother on business trips to Cape Town. 'The world says that a man, like an elephant, may graze where he will,' he told me, 'but some trees are poison, and this elephant ate from the wrong tree.'"

Solly picked up a bit of broken brick and threw it into the crumbling trench. "He said he didn't want me to make the same mistake." He took a deep breath. "He asked me to forgive him."

I shivered and hunched against the unfinished wall. The bricks still held the warmth of the day although the air was cooling quickly.

Solly sniffed loudly and wiped his nose. "But I didn't." He shifted, and a soft light from the kitchen window touched his face. It was twisted in grief. "I screamed at him and cursed him and accused him of destroying us all. He cried like a little child, and I wouldn't comfort him. Then he started to cough."

Solly was crying now. I wanted to say it would be all right, but I knew it wouldn't. It would never be all right. It would never be like Before.

He wiped his face on his arm. He had given me his only tissue, and it lay in a sodden ball in my fist. "Even in the hospital …"

I remembered the silent cry in Baba's eyes, the grip of his hand on my fingers.

Solly's shoulders trembled. "I turned away." He buried his face in his hands. "He was a good man, Sindi—a good man who made a terrible mistake. I just want to be like him. But I can't. I don't know how. I don't know how to take care of you and Jabu and Mama. I've tried to find a job, but no one wants to hire me. I'm too young. I'm not strong enough. I need money to rent the uniform. I'm worthless."

I knelt in the dirt and wrapped my arms around him. "You aren't worthless, Solly." His body was tense in my arms. "You aren't."

Solly closed his eyes and tilted his face to the stars. "I just want to be a man."

Chapter 27

The day we were to appear in court over Uncle Njabulo's challenge of Baba's will, Mama told us to wear our best.

I found Solly standing in front of the mirror, fingering Baba's suit.

"You look good," I said to his reflection. "Like a man."

"I wish it were as simple as putting on a suit."

Mama came in. "Oh!" She stared at him, but she didn't cry. After a few moments she nodded and went away again.

Pastor Oscar showed up with Mboti when we were ready to leave. "Mboti will stay here while you are gone," he announced. When Mama looked puzzled, Pastor Oscar cleared his throat. "In case any of your brother-in-law's friends should drop by for a visit."

Mama's eyes got big. "Of course," she stammered. "That would be ... very helpful."

Mboti settled on a chair under the jacaranda tree. Pastor Oscar got into the car with us. Besides being the one who had produced the will, he had witnessed it and would have to offer testimony that Baba was in his right mind.

"Of course he was in his right mind!" Solly muttered as we got into the car. "What kind of fool would let his no-good brother—"

"Solly," Mama said firmly. "Whatever your uncle has done, we must be respectful."

Pastor Oscar nodded approvingly and got in on the passenger side. Mama drove in silence. I sat in the back seat, squeezed between Solly and Jabu, and tried to pray, but "Dear God, dear God, dear God," was all I could find to say.

The shaded streets of Pretoria seemed like another world to Tembisa. We passed tall houses of brick and stone with wide porches and elegant gardens.

"They're all so old," Jabu said. Jabu liked everything to be the latest fashion.

Pastor Oscar nodded. "This city has been around for a long time. It was the capitol of the Transvaal Republic, you know. That was at the end of the nineteenth century before the Anglo-Boer War." It gave me a funny feeling in my stomach to think that black people only came here as servants when these houses were built.

Jabu looked more interested when we arrived in the city center where modern buildings loomed over the ornate remains of a faded past.

Mama found a parking place in Church Square. When the car doors were opened, the heat rushed in. Pretoria was at a lower altitude than Tembisa and hotter. The green lawn of the park spread out in front of us, dotted with people relaxing. Flowerboxes along the railing overflowed with summer color. A tall statue of Afrikaner president Paul Kruger gazed sternly down as though he would not approve of black people like us walking freely over the lawns.

"They should put a statue of Nelson Mandela here instead," I said.

Solly snorted. "Like they're going to do that."

"Well," I said, "the Palace of Justice was where he was tried and sent to prison."

We climbed the steps to the turreted Palace. Mandela did not get justice here. I hoped we would. But we didn't. Not there.

A guard shooed us away with a frown. "The high court doesn't meet here anymore." He directed us around the building, up Vermuelenstraat to a modern concrete-and-glass structure that Jabu liked much better. I would have liked to have seen the inside of a palace—especially the one where Mandela was tried.

"Hurry," Mama said. "We don't want to be late." But I wasn't in such a hurry to see Uncle Njabulo.

The lawyer Pastor Oscar had recommended greeted us in the corridor. He shook our hands and led us into the muffled quiet of the dark-paneled courtroom. Uncle Njabulo wasn't there. I breathed a little easier.

"Maybe he won't come," Jabu said bitterly as we filed into the front row of the public gallery and sat down.

Solly leaned forward and rested his elbows on his knees. His eyes swept uncomfortably this way and that. Mama stared ahead, her back straight, head high, as if nothing in that room interested her. Once her mobile phone vibrated. She looked at the number, but clicked it off without answering.

After forty-five minutes the bailiff called the case. A lawyer stood up at the table across the aisle. Mama glared at him. The man never glanced in our direction. "Your honor, I request an adjournment. My client has been delayed."

The judge in his black robe looked over his glasses. "Was he not told the time to be in court?"

"He was, your honor, but the distance from KwaZulu-Natal is great. Anything may have happened to delay him."

The judge looked at the clock in the back of the courtroom. "I can move your case further down the docket, but that's the best I can do for you." He made a notation on the papers in front of him, and the bailiff called the next case.

"What does it mean?" I whispered.

Mama looked at our lawyer. "It means God may have answered our prayers, doesn't it?"

Our lawyer was smiling broadly. "Could be."

It was nearly time for the midday recess when the judge asked, "Mr. Mbeke, has your client arrived?"

"No, your honor. He has not. I request an adjournment until tomorrow."

"Request denied. Case dismissed. This court is in recess until two p.m."

We all stood as the judge left the room.

I turned to Mama. "I don't understand."

Mama grinned. "It means, Sindi-wam, that your uncle did not choose to appear, and the case he brought to overturn your father's will is dismissed. Our house is our own and everything in it." She smiled and wiped a tear from her eye.

* * *

When we got home, Mboti said to me, "I'm going to take

a few things to Evelyn, S'bo, and the baby. I thought you might like to go along."

Jabu frowned. "Who's that?"

"Just some friends," Mboti said. "You're welcome to come too."

For one moment, I thought she might say yes, but then she shook her head. "I don't think so."

Mboti nodded. "Sindi?"

"I'd love to go."

We stopped by the church to pick up supplies. Evelyn was happy to see us. The baby had grown. He smiled and gurgled at me and swiped at my nose with his fat little hand.

"The test was negative?" Mboti asked.

"Yes!" The baby's mother glowed. "He's fine."

"Praise God! Let's thank him." Like the last time we were here, Mboti drew us into a circle to pray. Tears ran down Evelyn's cheeks—tears of happiness. I had a tiny glimpse of how people infected with HIV could still be full of joy.

* * *

"I need to make one more stop," Mboti said as we left Evelyn and S'bo's. "Do you mind?"

"Of course not. Do they have a baby?" I asked cheerfully.

"No, 'fraid not. And you should probably wait outside at this one. Mateus isn't quite ready to talk openly about his situation." He still carried a bag of vegetables from the church garden.

It was a small house of concrete blocks behind a crumbling wall on a narrow side street. The yard was overgrown with weeds. Turquoise paint clung in patches to the blocks. The trim might have once been black.

"Wait here," Mboti instructed. He knocked on the door. "Mateus? Mateus, are you here?" A sound came from inside, and Mboti let himself in. A sour smell of sickness seeped out when he opened the door.

I sat on the stoop to wait. Radios blared from cars passing on the main road. A group of children laughed and shouted as they kicked a worn football between cool-drink cans in the side street. I tried not to listen to the voices from the house.

"Have you gone for the test yet?" Mboti asked. "I'd be happy to take you to the clinic."

The mumbled response was lost in the noise of a passing bakkie. I plucked weeds from a crack in the concrete. Our visit with Evelyn, S'bo, and the baby had put me in a good mood. A boy slid around the corner of the house. His back was to me, but I recognized him instantly. My heart thumped in my chest. I didn't dare to move. He cocked his head toward the house as though he were listening to the conversation.

"How is your grandson doing?" came Mboti's voice from inside. "Is he able to help you?"

The boy turned, and I thought he was preparing to vault over the low wall, when he saw me and froze.

"Sindiswa?"

I swallowed. "Hello, Thabo."

"What are you doing here?"

I glanced at the closed door. "I ... I came with Mboti. He brought some vegetables from the church garden."

Thabo held his distance.

"I'm sorry your grandfather's sick."

He shrugged and tossed a stone at the wall. "He's not really sick. He's just old."

I tried to smile. "It's nice that he has you to help."

Thabo shrugged again, but he didn't look at me.

A harsh call came from the house. "Thabo! Get in here, boy." The voice broke off in a series of coughs that sounded to me like more than old age.

Thabo glanced at the street as though he might be thinking of running. I wouldn't have blamed him if he did. I didn't think his grandfather sounded very nice.

I stood up and moved away from the door. Thabo dropped the handful of pebbles he had been holding and wiped the dust from his hands on his shorts. He didn't say a word, but he gave me a wary look as he went in the door.

* * *

Mama's mobile rang while we were eating dinner. A frown wrinkled her face when she saw the number, but this time she answered. "Hello." Her frown deepened.

Jabu clicked the remote to mute the television.

"I see …" Mama said. "Of course … I'm sorry … This is an awkward time. I'm not sure we can come." The voice on the other end of the line continued. We waited. "I will think about it … Yes… Please express our condolences to Sisi Zanele."

Sisi Zanele?

Mama clicked her phone shut and sat staring at it for a long time before she spoke. "That was your Uncle Thulani. It appears that your Uncle Njabulo was not in court today because he rolled his bakkie on the road. He is dead."

"Dead?" Jabu said.

I thought of Pastor Oscar's words: One never knew what the future would bring. What was that Bible verse he quoted? Something about dying and after that … I shifted uncomfortably on my chair. God would judge Uncle Njabulo for what he had tried to do.

Chapter 28

There was an argument when school started up again the end of January and Jabu didn't want to go back.

"I'm making money braiding hair," she said.

"Is that what you plan to do the rest of your life?" Mama asked. "This is your matric year. You can't stop now."

"But my clients—" Jabu began.

"You can do them on Saturdays or after school." And that was the last word.

I hated to bring up skating when Mama was already upset. I tried to be casual about it when we were in the kitchen preparing the food. "Has Liselle called about lessons yet? They start next week, don't they?" Mama's shoulders stiffened, and I thought about all the times she hadn't answered her phone. "Shouldn't I get in some practice before then?"

Mama's hand paused in stirring the pot of pap. I held my breath. "We don't really have the money right now," she said slowly.

"I have a hundred rand," I put in quickly.

Mama turned and leaned against the cooker. Her eyes looked sad. "Sindi-wam, a hundred rand won't even pay for a week of daily practice, certainly not lessons. I'm sorry."

I opened my mouth to tell Mama about Ms. Etherington, but Mama raised her hand to silence me.

"Not right now, Sindi. We can talk about this later."

* * *

Mama didn't know when I bunked school. It was the first time in my life. Good little Sindi Khumalo. I went to school for the first week but by Tuesday of the second week I couldn't face it. I felt closed inside the crowded classroom, and the smell of dust mixed with turpentine made me queasy.

That day still felt like summer. The sun beat mercilessly, and the air was heavy with humidity. The sky was clear, but I knew there would be thunderstorms before evening.

After I put on my school uniform, I stuffed my skates and a change of clothes in my bag instead of my books. I said goodbye to Jabu at the school gate as usual, but as soon as she was out of sight, I headed for the taxi rank. The taxi took me to the rink in the northern suburbs where I wouldn't see MakaMboti or Andile. Liselle wouldn't be there or any of the other skaters— not on the public session at a distant rink. They would have finished their workouts and headed for school by now.

School—where I should be.

Guilt burrowed into my gut like a worm. I glanced sideways at the heavy woman next to me who balanced a large satchel on her lap. She didn't seem concerned about a girl in a school uniform, clutching a book bag. I had rehearsed a lie about being sent to my aunt whose husband had just been in an accident, but no one asked for it.

It took well over an hour to get to the rink in the rush-hour traffic. Other than Lake Placid, I had never been so far from home by myself. Mama had always been with me, or Jabu or Liselle if it was a competition. I might have asked the driver to let me out and flagged a taxi going the other way, but the thought of standing on the road in a strange part of the city, waiting for a taxi that wasn't already packed with commuters, was even more frightening than staying where I was.

The taxi stopped across from a large mall. I threw my satchel on my back and trudged across the hot parking lot toward the rink at the far end. *Don't hesitate. Don't look back.* I raised my chin a little higher. *Look confident,* I reminded myself, *and no one will question you.* I hoped I looked more confident than I felt.

I stopped in the toilets to change into a pair of stretch pants. A jacket would be nice when I reached the chill of the rink, but until then it would just draw attention on such a hot day. I folded my uniform small and stuffed it in the bottom of my bag.

The cold air of the rink hit my face when I stepped inside. The girl in the ticket box gave me a curious glance when I gave

her my money, but she didn't ask what I was doing there. The
rink was empty except for a woman in a blue tracksuit who
pushed her way around the outside barrier.

I set down my bag in a corner and jogged on the spot to
warm my muscles, then lifted one leg to rest my foot on the ledge.
The muscle inside my thigh screamed as it stretched. I counted
slowly to thirty and gradually the cramped muscle relaxed.

What if I have forgotten how to skate? I wondered. *What if my
body can't do this anymore?* I slid my foot down the ledge a few
inches, counted silently to thirty again and stretched further. *Don't
think about it. Just do it.*

My feet didn't slide as easily into the padded skating
boots as usual. I had grown over the summer. Soon I would need
new skates. I laced them loosely over the foot, trying not to pinch
too much, and then tightly around the ankle. I couldn't imagine
Mama paying for new skates. Would Ms. Etherington?

I stepped onto the ice and stroked around one end. My
feet hurt, but I didn't care. I had come here to skate. I bent my
knees and stroked harder. I glided past the woman in her rental
skates and did crossovers around the far end. Three turn. Back
crossovers. Right inside edge, crossover, left inside edge,
crossover. I circled the ice, skating practice patterns one after
another. As my speed increased, my mind numbed to the pain of
recent days, my body forgot to notice the cramps in my feet or
the tightness of my boots.

The music over the loudspeakers was loud and raucous—
something Solly would like. But the music in my head was all the
skating programs I had ever performed.

I'll be sore tonight, I thought with satisfaction, although I
would have been sorer if I hadn't done all that off-ice training.
Through the glass wall that separated the rink from the mall
corridor, a woman watched with a baby in a pushchair. A small
girl pressed her nose against the glass beside her.

I spent twenty minutes doing long deep edges and dance
steps before I even tried a spin. The rink blurred around me, and
when I felt myself perfectly centered, I pulled my arms and free
leg into my body and spun faster and faster. I stepped out of the

spin and glided backward on a long right outside edge. My shoulders were square, my back straight, and my arms extended in a graceful arch on either side. Liselle would be proud. The taste of salt was my first clue that I was crying.

I stepped forward, got up speed, turned backward at the far end of the ice for a few crossovers before turning forward and leaping into the air. I rose, rotated two and a half times, and landed in a perfect double-Axel jump. I was back. I could fly like a bird. I didn't have to crawl in the dirt. I threw back my head and laughed for joy.

The railing in the mall corridor was lined with people. They were all watching me. I laughed and waved. *Maybe I should even take a bow.* I turned and got ready for another jump.

"Sindiswa Khumalo! Where have you been?"

My head jerked around, throwing me off balance, and I fell with a splat on the ice. Lerato's mother was standing by the boards. I picked myself up and didn't dare to look at my audience on the other side of the glass. I skated slowly toward MakaLerato. My heart was beating hard, and it wasn't from exercise. What was I going to say to her? The lie about my aunt's husband having an accident wouldn't do any good now.

"We haven't seen you at practice in two months. No one picks up when I call your mother's mobile. I went by your house, and someone else is living there, of all things. They say they have been since last winter—before you even went to America! We have been so worried. It's as if you just dropped off the face of the earth. And now here you are at a completely different rink on the far side of the city in the middle of the day. Why aren't you at school?"

She stopped and for the first time seemed to expect an answer. I stared at her with my mouth gaping.

"You're bunking, aren't you?" she said at last.

I thought of telling her I was going to a private school that hadn't started yet, but I didn't think she would believe me.

She plopped on the nearest bench and wrapped her arms around herself against the cold. "As long as you're here, let's see what you're doing. Will your program be ready for the fall competition?"

I stared at her.

"Go on now. Let's see it. You don't need the music."

I took my starting position. I pivoted, turned, glided and jumped. I didn't even hear the rock music on the loudspeaker. I heard only the music in my head that told me when to jump or spin, step and glide. I got through it without falling.

"You haven't done it in a while, have you?" MakaLerato said, standing up and coming to the barrier. "It needs work, but I can see you have been training off the ice even if you haven't been showing up for practice. Or have you been bunking school?"

"This is the first time, MakaLerato. I swear."

"And it had better be the last!"

"Yes, ma."

She eyed me thoughtfully. "You have your reasons, I expect." When I didn't answer, she went on. "I could pick you up …"

I raised my eyes in panic. Mama would kill me if I gave her our address.

"Let's say … the taxi rank in Kempton, Saturday morning at nine."

I shook my head. "I don't think …"

MakaLerato ignored my objections. "The traffic won't be bad at that hour, and this rink shouldn't be too crowded if we get here right when they open. You can have a good skate, and I'll take you back. I'm not a coach, but that can't be helped." A tiny spark of hope began to glow inside me.

She glanced at her watch. "There's just time for a bite of lunch before I take you home—or to the taxi rank if you prefer," she added quickly when I started to protest. She shook her head and gave a disgusted snort. "It's a crime for someone as talented as you not to be skating."

Chapter 29

I made it back to the school gate in time to meet Jabu. She didn't ask about my day. It was a good thing, or I probably would have told her I had bunked school for skating and that I had run into MakaLerato and she wanted to help. The joy of it all bubbled inside me.

James and Thabo were already leaning against the wall of the Community Chat when we got home. They probably bunked school too.

I had just changed out of my school uniform and hidden my skates in the bottom of the wardrobe when a rattling began at the gate. Mama was still at work. Who knew where Solly was? At least I hadn't seen him hanging out at the Community Chat.

I went to the gate and called through the crack. "Who is it?"

"Sindi? Is that you? It's me—Mboti. Do you want to go visiting with me this afternoon?"

I threw open the gate. "Sure." Today I felt as if I could do anything.

Mboti looked pleased. "Evelyn told me about a woman who's sick. She lives in the informal settlement not far from where I found you."

My flesh went cold. Mboti's voice seemed to echo down a long tunnel.

"I know you don't want to go into the settlement, but the woman's daughter is named Takalani." He hesitated. "I thought it might be your friend."

I stared at him. "Takalani?"

"Sindi, who is it?" Jabu called from the doorway.

When I didn't answer, she came down the steps toward us.

Mboti only glanced at her. "I'm going there now. I'm kind of in a hurry, but I thought you might want to come."

I swallowed.

"She could use a friend."

I didn't want to go into the settlement. The muscles of my chest seemed to squeeze so tight that I couldn't breathe when I thought of what almost happened there.

Mboti waited.

But what if my mother were so sick? I hid when Takalani was in trouble before. Was I going to go on hiding? I glanced toward James outside the Community Chat. He was here. He wasn't lurking in the settlement to grab me. And I wouldn't be alone. Mboti would be there.

I took a deep breath. "I'll go."

Jabu had come up behind us. "Where to?" she demanded.

"To the informal settlement. A girl from my class last year … her mother is very sick," I tried to explain.

"Oh no, you don't! You're not going there alone."

"She'll be with me," Mboti said.

Jabu shook her beaded braids. "She is not *your* sister."

Mboti rolled his eyes. "All right. So you come too."

I don't think that was what Jabu had in mind, but Mboti pulled her after us. We barely had time to lock the house.

We stopped at the church where Mboti handed Jabu a packet of adult nappies. Her eyes opened so wide I could see the whites all around, and I thought she was about to back out. I picked up a sack of vegetables from the community garden and a bag of powdered soup and tinned meat. Mboti swung his satchel over his shoulder. I glimpsed Thabo and James coming up the street as Mboti locked the gate. I stood between Mboti and Jabu and tried to pretend they weren't there.

Beyond the T in the road by the church stretched the shacks of the informal settlement. The smell of charcoal fires and roasting mealies greeted us. Other smells, not so nice, reminded me of the last time I had been here.

Mboti plunged down an alley. Jabu wrinkled her nose and picked her way around a heap of trash as she followed. Mboti looked back and waited for me. I took a deep breath and stepped off the pavement.

"Mboti! Good to see you." Many people smiled and greeted him. He greeted them by name. He must have spent a lot of time in the settlement to have so many friends. "This is Jabulile and Sindiswa." He introduced us over and over, and I began to feel as if I would have many friends watching out for me if I came back. But there were others who eyed Mboti warily and, like Andile, stepped out of the way rather than greet us.

We went down narrow alleys between the shacks.

"What is that stench?" Jabu demanded as we approached the drainage ditch. My heart beat harder the nearer we came. We passed the old woman. The tiny girl had grown. She lay on the mat fast asleep.

"*Molo, umakhulu*," Mboti greeted the old woman respectfully. "Did you sleep well?"

"I slept well," she replied and smiled with pleasure at his attention. She looked at me like she was trying to remember where she had seen me.

I slid my grocery packets over my wrists so I could put my palms together and bow my head. "*Molo, umakhulu*," I murmured.

The shacks closest to the ditch had washed away in last week's heavy rain, but the broken bits were already being recycled into new shacks in the same spots even though the rains were nowhere near finished for the season. They would surely be washed away again.

We turned left into a tiny courtyard surrounded by shacks. A woman leaned over a plastic basin by the single tap in the center of the courtyard. She swished clothes in soapy water.

"*Sawubona, Mama*," Mboti greeted her. "I understand there is someone here who is sick."

The woman's eyes slid from us to the flimsy building on the right. Its lower walls were sodden where last week's rain must have brought the ditch to the door.

I hung back as Mboti knocked on the post beside the open door. Maybe this wasn't Takalani's house. Maybe it was just a stranger, and I wouldn't have to go in. But to Mboti no one was just a stranger. Everyone deserved a friend.

Something moved inside the shack. A face appeared in the doorway.

"Takalani!" I called.

She blinked when she saw me, and a little of the worry left her face. Mboti explained why we had come. "She won't wake up," Takalani told him. "I tried to give her tea, but I can't wake her."

Mboti pushed past the girl into the tiny shack. He set his satchel on the damp ground and knelt by the low bed. I followed Takalani into the room and put down my grocery bags. The room was so deep in shadow that I could barely make out the thin form under the blankets. I wasn't sure if the stench of urine came from the bed or from the heap of dirty linen by the door.

Jabu took one step into the room, swayed, and bolted with her hand over her mouth.

Takalani knelt and picked up a dented tin cup. "Drink it, Ma. Please drink it. You need liquids."

Mboti shook his head. "She needs a doctor." He pulled out his mobile phone and pressed some numbers. When he had asked for an ambulance, he turned to me. "I'll go out to the road to show them the way. You'll be all right here with Takalani." I wasn't sure if it was a statement or a question. Mboti left us alone. He stopped outside to say something to Jabu.

"Mboti!" she called after him.

But his answer came from halfway out of the courtyard. "I have to meet the ambulance to show them the way."

I turned back to the shadows of the bed and stared at the woman, but it seemed to be my father who lay there instead. Takalani sat on a low stool, still as stone, watching her mother's thin chest rise and fall oh, so slightly. Sometimes I thought it had stopped. Sometimes I thought it moved just a little, and then sometimes I wasn't sure. I pulled up another stool and sat beside Takalani. That's what friends did.

She didn't stir at the sound of voices outside.

"Maybe that's the paramedics," I said, going to the door. It wasn't.

"So this is where you were rushing off to," James said. Thabo looked like he was trying to hide behind him. When he saw me, he drew back. *Don't tell! Don't tell!* his eyes screamed.

James tossed a stone back and forth from one hand to the other. The woman who had been washing her clothes poured the water from her basin onto a straggly plant by her door and retreated inside. The courtyard was empty except for Jabu, sitting on a bench breathing slowly and deliberately as if she was trying not to be sick again.

"Are you a *friend* of Takalani?" James jerked his head at the shack behind me. Something seemed to stir in his mind. "You were looking for her before, weren't you?"

When I didn't answer, he went on. "I wouldn't go in there if I were you. You know, her mother has AIDS."

"Does she?" I asked, angry at his ignorance. "When did you become her doctor?"

James seemed to think that was funny.

"You can't get HIV from casual contact," I said.

James leered and stepped closer. "But you can get it from being raped," he whispered. "No drainage ditch here to jump into."

Suddenly I didn't feel so confident. Jabu looked up and frowned.

James tossed the stone high in the air and neatly caught it behind his back. "That's how Takalani got it, you know. Her stepfather thought sex with a virgin would cure him. Didn't do the old fool any good, did it, Thabo?" He grabbed Thabo around the neck, wrestled his head down and pounded it with his fist. "Did it, Thabo?"

"No, James," Thabo gasped. "No good."

James let go. Thabo fell back, gasping for breath. James slapped his thigh and laughed like it was a big joke. My knees felt weak with horror, and I felt for the doorpost beside me. Thabo rubbed his neck and looked at me as if he was as afraid of James as I was.

James paced. The rock passed from one hand to the other. I didn't think I would be quick enough if he decided to throw it. "So Takalani's not a virgin anymore," he said. "Shame."

James hurled the rock past my head. It thumped against the flimsy wall of the shack. I jumped. The rock dropped to the ground with a dull thud. "But then you hang out with that Mboti fellow, don't you? And everyone knows he has the virus. He doesn't even try to hide it. He has no shame."

I glared at him. "HIV isn't a shame," I said loudly. "It's a virus."

James made a lewd gesture. "But how did he get it?"

I realized suddenly that I didn't know how Mboti got HIV. It was hard to imagine him going from girl to girl like Makatso, but then, he said he had changed. People made mistakes. Jabu had. I felt Takalani's presence in the doorway beside me.

"Maybe it doesn't matter how a person got the virus," I said, fixing my eyes on Thabo. "Maybe what matters is the choices they're making right now, like choosing to take responsibility for their actions; to protect their health and those they love; to tell the truth like Mboti and not hide behind their ignorance like Makatso." I was tired of hiding, tired of keeping secrets.

Thabo blinked hungrily as if he wanted to believe. Takalani stepped through the doorway and stood beside me. I twined my fingers in hers and squeezed. She squeezed back.

"What do you know?" James taunted. "Your father died, didn't he? He probably had AIDS too."

His words tore my heart. How I missed Baba! Takalani squeezed my hand. Jabu stood up from the bench and came to stand at my other side. What I had feared would happen had happened. James had guessed the secret. He wouldn't keep it quiet, of that I was certain. But I wasn't alone.

"Hey, Thabo," James shouted over his shoulder, "Sindiswa's family is infected. That's why she isn't afraid of being friends with these people." He scooped up a loose hunk of concrete from the courtyard. "Let's get 'em!" He drew back his hand to throw.

Thabo didn't move. "Leave them alone, James."

I jerked my eyes from James to Thabo.

James turned slowly. "What did you say?"

Thabo looked at me. He took a deep breath and looked back at James. "I said, leave them alone." His voice was loud and firm. I couldn't see James's face, only the back of his head. "You're acting stupid," Thabo went on. "Stupid like Makatso."

"Why you—"

Just then I heard Mboti's voice. "It's through here."

He led the paramedics into the courtyard. When I looked back, James was gone. But Thabo wasn't. He stayed while the paramedics lifted the sick woman gently onto the stretcher. He walked with us as we followed them back through the twisted alleys of the settlement to the place where they had left the ambulance, watching every move Mboti made.

"I'll come and see you tomorrow," Mboti promised as he helped Takalani into the back of the ambulance with her mother. Her eyes were very big and very frightened. "Don't worry. We'll take care of you."

I clung to Jabu's hand and waved as the ambulance lurched down the road and turned a corner. Jabu began to shake. Her sweat reeked of vomit.

She grasped Mboti's arm. "I don't want to die like this." She hiccupped. "I have to know! I want to get tested."

Mboti slid an arm around her shoulders. "We'll go tomorrow," he said.

I took his other hand and looked up into his calm face. "I want to go too," I said.

Mboti nodded. I looked around, but Thabo was gone.

Chapter 30

I wanted to bunk school again, but Mboti wouldn't let me. We left as soon as classes let out. We took a taxi to the clinic at Tembisa Hospital—the three of us, Mboti, Jabu, and me. There was a line outside the clinic. So many people.

"Have they all come for testing?" I whispered in Mboti's ear.

He shook his head. "Some are coming back for medicine." He smiled and nodded at several whom he seemed to recognize, but mostly we stood quietly, waiting. We were alone in the crowd, surrounded by people as alone as we were. We all carried the same secret, but we didn't share it. If we didn't look each other in the eye, we could still pretend that no one knew, no one guessed the fear, the pain, or the regret.

The line of people filed into the clinic, and we gradually moved from hot sun with a slight breeze to the stifling air of a confined space. At last we reached the reception desk.

"Name?" The sister behind the counter was looking at Jabu, but Jabu seemed to have forgotten how to talk.

I stepped forward. "I'm Sindiswa Khumalo, and this is my sister Jabulile. We both want to get tested."

"It's just to put our minds at ease," Jabu put in quickly. "She's worried, you know. I don't think she's sick or anything."

The sister wrote down our names. "Sit over there. I'll call you when the counselor is ready."

Mboti guided us to the long hard benches. A lady sat next to us. She leaned forward and untied her baby from her back. The baby looked up at me with serious brown eyes framed with black curly lashes. Her mother nodded politely and looked away. She didn't invite conversation.

I slumped in my seat. I might meet this same woman on the street tomorrow, but I could never say to her, "Didn't I see you at the clinic yesterday? How are you? How's the baby?" If we met, we would pass each other without a word or a nod so that someone else on the street—someone who wasn't part of this silent, clinic club, someone who hadn't bothered to find out his status and so was secure in his ignorance—so that someone didn't guess our secret.

Mboti sat on the other side of Jabu. She clung to his hand. Would it be easier for him if she were positive too? I didn't think so. He loved her. I mean, he really loved her. He didn't just want to sleep with her.

A large woman with grey in her short, fluffy hair left the desk and came toward us.

"You've come for testing?" she asked.

Jabu nodded.

"Follow me."

Jabu seemed reluctant to let go of Mboti's hand. "I'll wait here," he said. "You'll be all right." He patted her hand and at last she let go.

The woman led us down a long, narrow corridor. People came and went quietly from doorways on either side. When we reached an open door, the woman gestured for me to enter. She started to lead Jabu to another door.

"Please. Can't we stay together?" I wasn't sure if I asked for my sake or for Jabu's.

The woman looked from one to the other. "There are confidentiality issues, but if that's what you want, it's your choice."

Jabu took a deep breath and nodded. The counselor in the little room was turned away, pinning a poster to the board behind her. She looked up when we came in. It was MakaLerato.

Jabu gasped and for a moment I thought she would turn and run.

"Sindi! Jabu!" MakaLerato looked surprised and pleased to see us before she remembered where we were. "If you would rather see someone else, I can arrange it."

"No, MakaLerato. I would rather see you," I said. Suddenly it seemed terribly important to talk to someone real with a life outside a sterile clinic room. I sat down and pulled Jabu after me. "The sister said about confidentiality. That means you can't tell anyone, right?"

"That's right, Sindi. Whatever happens here is your secret. You must choose whom you can trust with it."

"Then I trust you."

MakaLerato didn't let on that she had seen me at the ice rink the day before and neither did I. She sat at the desk and took out a little white card, which she began to fill in. "I need to ask you: why do you want to be tested?"

I had carried this secret too long. I was sick of *Don't tell*. Jabu stared at her hands twisting nervously in her lap.

"Our father died of AIDS in December," I said. I knew MakaLerato wasn't supposed to show emotion, but I could see the sudden understanding in her eyes. "It was right after the ice show. I helped take care of him, cleaning his sores and all." I shook my head. "I never wore gloves."

MakaLerato leaned back in her chair. "What do you know about HIV, Sindi?"

"I know …" What did I know? Suddenly I couldn't think of anything except my fear for myself and for Jabu. "I know … what they told us at school about babies getting it from their mothers, and about sharp things. I know you can get it from …" Takalani's hunched shoulders came into my mind. "… from being raped." Mboti would make sure she got what she needed.

MakaLerato spoke quietly. "Sindi, has anyone ever touched you inappropriately?"

I thought of James and the other boy in the settlement and what they would have done if I hadn't thrown us all into the drainage ditch. "No. Never." I took a deep breath. "But sometimes people get it from blood like when you're taking care of a sick person."

MakaLerato nodded. She spoke to me, but I was glad Jabu could hear. "The other thing that you need to know about HIV is that it is not a death sentence. People with HIV in their blood need to take good care of themselves—get plenty of sleep, exercise, eat healthy foods like fruits and vegetables. Those are things that all young people need to do whether they have HIV or not."

My head nodded stiffly on my neck.

"If you *have* contracted HIV, you must also be careful not to be re-infected. Always wear gloves when you touch body fluids or open sores whether you know the person's status or not. And when you get older and are ready to be with a boy, you will want to use a condom."

My cheeks flushed hot when she talked about "being with a boy." I didn't dare to look at Jabu.

"In the meantime," MakaLerato went on, "there are medicines we can give a person with HIV to prevent infections. It's not HIV that kills you, you know. It's the other diseases."

She was kind and gentle, and it felt good to be able to talk about the secret at last. "I know," I said. "Baba had pneumonia."

MakaLerato shook her head and clicked her tongue sympathetically. "Unfortunately, pneumonia is very common among people with HIV disease. So is tuberculosis, what we call 'TB.' HIV destroys the T-cells in a person's blood that fight the other diseases. But if you're careful—take your medicine and live a healthy lifestyle—you can live a very long time with HIV. You can grow up, fall in love, and have children of your own if that's what you want—even with HIV."

The tight knot in my stomach began to loosen.

"Do you have any questions?"

I looked at Jabu. She had been sitting quietly while MakaLerato and I talked. Her shoulders were hunched, but her eyes were glued to MakaLerato's face as if her life depended on every word. Tiny beads of sweat clung to the fine hairs on her cheeks. She glanced up when she saw me looking at her, but she didn't tell me any questions to ask. I looked back at MakaLerato and shook my head.

"Would you like to be tested now?" she asked.

"Yes, please."

She took a paper packet from a blue-and-white box on the little table in front of her and ripped it open.

"Give me your finger." She wiped it with a swab that smelled of alcohol and made me think of Baba in the hospital. I bit my lip and blinked hard while she poked me with a little metal stick. A bright ball of red swelled on my fingertip. She used a small white plastic tube to suction blood from the end of my finger and smear it onto the slide from the packet.

"We always do a second test, just to be sure," MakaLerato explained as she took a packet from a different box. "But we do it at the same time so I don't have to prick you twice." She smiled as if she thought the tears in my eyes were for the prick on my finger instead of for my father lying under the ground between the cattle kraal and the big tree far away in KwaZulu-Natal.

She wiped my finger with another alcohol swab and added a cotton ball. "Just press that tight until the bleeding stops," MakaLerato said.

"We've missed you at the rink." She marked my name on each slide. "You know, if money is a problem, the club could do a fundraiser." I couldn't imagine Mrs. Brodowski agreeing to that. MakaLerato must have realized how unlikely it was, because she added hopefully, "Or maybe we could look for a sponsor."

A huge weight had fallen off my back as the blood was drawn from my finger. I didn't know the results yet, but I had gotten the test. Now Sindi Skater stirred impatiently from her hiding place in the heel of my shoe.

"I have a sp—" I began before I caught myself.

MakaLerato looked up while her pen hovered over the slide. Jabu raised her head slowly as if bringing her mind back from a distant place.

"You have a sponsor?" MakaLerato asked slowly.

I stared at the desktop. All my secrets were coming out at once. I chewed my lip. I took a deep breath. "Ms. Etherington … at Lake Placid … She wanted to sponsor me. She's the one who gave me that beautiful dress. But I couldn't stay! Baba was so sick. I was worried about Mama. My family needed me."

MakaLerato folded her hands in front of her. "I see." Jabu's eyes drifted back to her lap. MakaLerato watched her, then turned back to me. "Perhaps things have changed now. Perhaps it is time for you to pursue your own dreams."

Was it too late? Sindi Skater poised like a bird on the tip of a branch ready to soar once more. Would Mac take me back? Would Ms. Etherington still think I was worth investing in?

MakaLerato set the slides with my blood on the little white card. "We'll know the results in fifteen minutes," she said. "You can go back to the waiting room. I'll call you when it's time."

I nodded. The only way to know was to write them—Mac and Ms. Etherington. I was glad I had spent so much time training off-ice. My excursion to the rink the other day showed I was ready. I looked hopefully at MakaLerato. Nothing could stop me now, not even HIV.

Jabu didn't move.

MakaLerato waited. "Would ... you like to be tested too?" she asked at last.

Jabu pursed her lips together. She didn't take her eyes off the floor, but her head bobbed in several short, quick nods.

MakaLerato looked at me. "Sindi, perhaps you should wait outside." I started to stand.

"No!" Jabu grabbed my hand. "I've had enough of secrets in this family. I want Sindi to stay." I sat back down. Jabu's breath came fast and shallow.

MakaLerato pulled out a second white card. "Why do you want to be tested, Jabulile?"

Jabu didn't answer.

"Is it because of your parents?"

Jabu shook her head. "I ... I slept with a boy." She hesitated. "I know he sleeps around. I know it was stupid not to use a condom, but it was my first time. I wasn't prepared. He said it was better without. And I trusted him." Bitterness curdled her voice. "I don't want Sindi to make the same mistake."

MakaLerato sighed a deep sigh as if she had heard this story many times before, but still felt its pain stabbing into her own heart. She reached into a large box on her desk and pulled out a handful of condoms in little paper packets. "Take these," she said. She took Jabu's hand in both her own as she gave them to her. "But you must understand that condoms don't work all the time. Sometimes they come off. Sometimes they break. Sometimes they have tiny holes in them that let the virus through just because they have been in the box too long, or the storage place has been too hot. It's better not to trust a condom." Her eyes flitted from Jabu to me and back again. "It's better to wait for the right man—one who will be faithful to you alone for a lifetime."

Jabu looked at her doubtfully, and MakaLerato squeezed her hand in both of hers.

"I know, I know," MakaLerato said. "There aren't many men around here who are willing to be faithful, but they're worth waiting for. You're worth it." She smiled at me again. "Both of you are. You aren't a plaything to be tossed away when he's done. You're not a maid to clean his house, prepare his food, and bear his children while he flits from lover to lover. You're a valuable human being. The Bible says you're made in the image of God just as he is."

MakaLerato didn't take her eyes from Jabu's face. Hope showed there, like a newly hatched butterfly, slowly stretching its damp and crumpled wings. "Whether you've got HIV from this boy you slept with or not, you can make a new beginning. We'll treat the virus if you have it and, if not, you'll learn from the experience." She shook her head. "You don't owe anyone your body. It's yours to keep and present to the one who will love you and be true to you for a lifetime."

I could see in Jabu's eyes that she wanted to believe what MakaLerato said. She wanted to believe she could start again. I thought of the blue vase and Mama's shattered dreams. Even a wonderful man like my father wasn't a guarantee. I thought of Mboti waiting outside. He said he had learned from his mistakes, that finding God had made a difference in his life. Was he now the sort of man who could be true to a woman for a lifetime?

"Do you want to be tested now?" MakaLerato asked.

Jabu straightened her shoulders and held out her finger. "Yes, please."

Chapter 31

We were serious as we climbed into the taxi. The tiny throb of my pricked finger was beginning to fade. Although I wouldn't have said it before, I realized now that I had expected to leave elated with good news. Instead we waited silently for the other seats to fill with discharged hospital patients, visitors, or outpatients who had finished at the clinic like us. No one talked much. There was nothing we could say in front of strangers.

An invisible bubble surrounded me. Sounds and voices seemed to come from far away through miles of water or thick jelly. I glanced sideways at Jabu. She gripped my hand on one side and Mboti's on the other. I tried to smile my encouragement to her, but it was harder than smiling for the judges at a skating competition. I looked away. We had wanted to know. Now we both knew.

"I'll come with you," Mboti had said. "It will be better if you aren't alone when you tell your mother."

The taxi wound along the narrow lanes at this end of Tembisa. It bounced over speed bumps. The journey took a long time with the late-afternoon traffic. Mama would be home when we got there.

We left the taxi and walked up the street past the Community Chat. Jabu didn't even look to see if Makatso was in his usual hangout.

"Thank you for coming, Mboti," I said as Jabu put her key in the lock and opened the gate. He smiled, and I knew he was trying as hard as I was to be encouraging.

"Where have you been?" Mama demanded as soon as we stepped into the lounge. "I get home from work, and no one is here. Dinner isn't even started. And did you do your homework before you went gallivanting around?"

I didn't say anything. Neither did Jabu.

Mama continued her scolding. "What has gotten into you girls? You aren't going to turn out to be as irresponsible as your brother, are you?"

"Mrs. Khumalo," Mboti put in. "We need to talk."

She stopped. Her eyes went from one to another, and she must have realized we had something serious to say.

"Let's sit down," Mboti said, and you might have thought he was the host instead of the guest.

We sat. I couldn't look at my mother. I stared down at the coffee table instead. The little blue-and-white vase I had given Mama for Christmas stood on a doily in the center. A handful of daisies smiled from it. It looked kind of pretty, and more than that—hopeful. I looked up.

"Mrs. Khumalo," Mboti said. "I know that you know about HIV. You know that it isn't a death sentence. You know that even though the immune system can be seriously compromised, with exercise, good nutrition, and the right medications a person can live many healthy and productive years." He sounded as if he had already memorized the little booklet MakaLerato had given us, but I guess it wasn't the first time he had read it. "I myself—"

Mama's eyes were steely as she interrupted. "If you have infected my daughter, young man—"

"Mama, please." Jabu looked more confident than I had seen her since the news. "Mboti hasn't touched me." I wondered if she would tell Mama about Makatso, but she didn't. After her outburst she shrank back into the cushions of the loveseat as if she wanted to disappear.

Solly came in. He leaned his tall frame against the doorpost and listened.

Mboti glanced at him and continued as though Mama had never interrupted. "I myself have known for several years that I am HIV positive. I made a lot of mistakes in the past. Since I got involved in the support group at the church, I've learned not only how to eat right and take my medicines. I've learned to control my behavior, to choose what is right and not just what my body wants at the moment. I've learned to know God, Mrs. Khumalo."

Mama's eyes darted from him to Jabu and back. "Why are you telling me this? There must be someone else. Oh, my God, you were raped! I'll kill him! I'll kill whoever did this to you!" Her voice rose shrilly.

Solly stepped forward, fists clenched.

Jabu put a hand on Mama's arm. "No, Mama." She shook her head. "I'm not infected."

I leaned forward. "Mama, please!"

She looked quickly from one to the other of us. "Then why are you talking like this? Tell me why!"

"It's not Jabu, Mama." My voice was tight in my throat— so tight the words were little more than a whisper. "It's me."

All the steely hardness melted out of her. Solly knelt on the floor as though his legs had gone weak. Mama's cheeks sagged, and she looked as old as she had that day when she tried to fit together the pieces of the broken vase. "Sindi-wam?"

I glanced at Solly. "I probably got it from nursing Baba. Remember those sores he had? He hadn't been tested, and we didn't know we needed to be careful. Now I have the virus in my blood. That's why it's so important to be tested. Don't you see? I needed to know. I didn't want to be careless and infect someone I loved." I didn't mean it to be an accusation, but after the words were out, I realized that they were.

I don't know at what point I started to cry, but I found myself in my mother's arms being cuddled like a baby. "Oh, Sindi, Sindi-wam," she crooned and rocked me back and forth. Tears rolled down her cheeks and got all mixed up with mine.

I could hear Jabu sobbing quietly. "It should have been me. It should have been me."

"Hush," Mboti comforted her. His head was bent over hers, and he touched her chin with the tip of his finger. "You have a second chance. Don't waste it."

We sat that way a long time. I leaned against my mother's shoulder and gazed at the little vase on the table. It wasn't the vase her madam had given her; it was different, but it was still pretty. Our lives would never be what they had been Before, but they could still be good lives. I looked at Mboti with my sister. They could be very good lives.

"Mama," I whispered. "I want to go back to America."

She drew back and stared at me. "What?"

"There's a woman there who offered to sponsor me. She'll pay all my skating expenses. Only I have to tell her the truth. Mac, too, my coach. And Jenni—I can't stay with her family and not tell them. I am tired of hiding, tired of secrets."

Mama frowned. "Maybe they won't want you if they know the truth."

I looked away from Mama's worried eyes, down at the little blue-and-white vase on the coffee table. Maybe they wouldn't. "Someone believes in me, Mama," I said slowly. "It's still me even with this virus in my blood. If I live a healthy lifestyle—eat right, exercise—the virus shouldn't make a difference for many years to come. There's no reason why I should stop skating, and this is my chance."

Mama pushed back my braids and caressed my cheek. "I believe in you, Sindi-wam. You'll make us proud." She looked up at Mboti and took a deep breath. "When does that HIV support group you talk about meet? Maybe it's time I started living my life again."

Chapter 32

Dear Mac,

I hope you are fine.

My father passed in December. This summer has been difficult for my family. I haven't skated as much as I would like, but if Ms. Etherington still wants to sponsor my training, I am ready to come to America. She should know before she decides that my father had AIDS. I recently learned that I have HIV in my blood too. I am healthy, and I promise to work very hard and take good care of my body. I believe that I can be a good investment for her.

Sincerely yours,
Sindiswa Khumalo

Ms. Etherington must have been best friends with the ambassador or something because I had my student visa in record time. "What about the HIV?" I asked Mac when he telephoned to make travel arrangements.

He laughed. "Amanda just took it as a bigger challenge," he said. " 'We'll show them what this girl can do, HIV or no HIV!' "

I hoped he was right. There were moments when I doubted and wondered why this had to happen to me. What if the virus multiplied too fast in my blood? What if I got sick? Worse, what if I made someone else sick?

It was Mboti who steadied me. "I know you, Sindi. You will be careful. You will take your medications. You will be fine."

Mboti believed in me. I had to believe in myself.

In less than two weeks I was on my way.

I called Liselle a few days before I left. My heart felt like it had slipped up into my throat making it hard to talk. "Hello, Liselle. It's me. Sindi."

"Sindi? Is it really you? We've missed you so much. When are you coming back to the rink? "

I took a deep breath. She wasn't mad. "I'm not. At least, not to stay. But I'd like to come and say goodbye to everyone." I told her all about Ms. Etherington and moving to Lake Placid to train. I didn't say anything about the past two months. "Just because you aren't keeping secrets doesn't mean you have to tell everyone everything." That was what MakaLerato had said.

Lerato and her mother met me in the parking lot the day I went back to the rink so we could go in together. I don't think her mother had told Lerato anything about why I hadn't been there.

"It's your secret," she had said to me. "You must choose whom you trust enough to tell."

But Lerato didn't ask questions. She just took my hand and welcomed me back. I could have trusted Lerato with my secret. She didn't chatter like Nicola, and I was pretty sure she would stand by me.

* * *

Clouds were building for the usual afternoon thunderstorm as Mama drove us to the airport. Lake Placid in February would be a lot colder than Jozi.

"Be sure and send us pictures of the snow," Jabu said. "And I bought you these." She stuck a couple of her favorite fashion magazines into my carry-on. "So you don't forget South Africa."

"I won't forget," I said as the familiar streets rolled past.

Mama's phone rang while we were walking in from the parking garage. She checked the number before she answered. "Yes, yes. We're coming."

Mboti walked ahead, lugging my suitcase. Solly pulled the other after him. The two were becoming good friends as they worked together on the room in the back yard after school. The walls were higher than my head now. Pastor Oscar said he knew where they could get some used panels cheap for the roof. Makatso didn't seem to be around much, and that was just fine with me.

On Saturday morning Solly and Mboti hadn't worked on the room. When they showed up at lunchtime, I asked Solly where they'd been. He mumbled something I couldn't hear. Later he pulled me aside in the back yard. "We went to the clinic, okay?"

My face must have showed my confusion.

"I'm fine," he explained. "I just didn't want to make a big deal. Not in front of Mama."

"You were tested."

He nodded.

I hugged him. "I'm glad you're fine."

"You're not mad?"

"Why would I be mad? Your being positive wouldn't change my status."

Solly hugged me back.

In the airport parking garage Mama clicked her phone shut. "Lerato and her mother will be waiting for us at international departures," she said.

MakaLerato had given me her business card when we left the clinic. I was glad Mama had called the phone number on it. The two of them went to lunch. Mama didn't get home until late, but when she did, she seemed almost like her old self. She talked to MakaLerato on the phone every day after that. On Thursday they went together to the HIV support group at church. That night Mama watched a movie with us in the lounge instead of hiding in the bedroom.

The traffic stopped to let us cross the road between the parking garage and the terminal.

Lerato burst through the door with her mother grinning behind her. A silver balloon bobbed from Lerato's wrist. "Sindi! I'm so excited!" She threw her arms around me. "You have to write on Facebook every day and post pictures of all the famous skaters you meet."

"I will," I promised.

Lerato dragged me through the door into the terminal where a whole crowd was waiting. Kobus and Mariki held up a banner that read, "Good Luck, Sindi!" Liselle, Nicola, and the other skaters held bunches of balloons. Pastor Oscar had brought MakaMboti, Evelyn, and S'bo. Takalani stood shyly to one side holding S'bo's baby, who kept trying to grab the balloons.

"She's staying with them," Mboti whispered in my ear. "And she's back in school. Her mother's responding well to treatment."

It was good to see my friends again. I needed friends to support me—"a community," Mboti had said. Mac had talked to Jenni's family for me. They were as supportive as Ms. Etherington so I wouldn't need to live in the dorm. There were days when I still grieved that I had this virus, and feared what it would do to me some day in the future, but I wasn't going to let keeping secrets isolate me again.

"It's time to go," Mama said.

"Goodbye, Sindi." Lerato brushed away a tear as she hugged me.

Nicola threw her arms around my neck. "I wanted to bring you flowers, but Mom said they would wilt before you got to America." Nicola was still my friend. Maybe someday I would be able to trust her with my secret.

"Good luck, Sindi," Mariki said when I reached her. "Make South Africa proud." And I was pretty sure she really meant it.

"Don't worry about your family," Mboti said. "They'll be taken care of." He held up a hand, his fingers laced in Jabu's. She smiled shyly at him, and her face glowed with contentment.

Pastor Oscar embraced me. "Shall we pray before you go?" My skating friends looked at each other uncertainly. Mariki blushed as if praying were something embarrassing to do in public, but Pastor Oscar laid his hands on my head. Mboti reached a hand to my shoulder. Evelyn and S'bo each took a hand. Takalani took S'bo's hand, and soon even the skaters joined in the circle.

"Most gracious heavenly Father," Pastor Oscar prayed. "Be a father to this child. Protect her on her journey. Guide her feet in a strange land. Comfort her family left behind." My mother sniffled behind me. "Keep them strong and healthy. Draw us ever closer to you, and make us one in community with your Son. To him be the glory forever and ever."

Mboti, Evelyn, and S'bo joined him, saying "Amen," and the others echoed it. When I looked up, Mariki was gazing at Pastor Oscar with hungry eyes.

Pastor Oscar hugged me again. "A present for you," he whispered, pressing a small book into my hand. "It's a message from your Father."

I looked at the cover. *New Testament,* it said. *The Gospel of Jesus Christ.* I looked back at Pastor Oscar. "Thank you. I promise to read it."

I hugged my mother one last time. "I love you, Nyoni," she whispered. "I believe in you." She squeezed my shoulders."

I waved to the others. Then I passed through the gate to follow my dream. I might lose an edge and tumble to the ice. It might hurt, but with the help of my friends I would get up, and I would keep skating.

The End

Things to Talk About

A book club is a good way to talk about books with others. Here are some questions you might want to discuss after you have read *Keeping Secrets*. If you don't have a book club, there are lots of online resources to help you start one. Or you can go to the discussion page on my website (www.leannehardy.net) and start a conversation there. I would love to hear from you.

1. How is Sindi's world like or unlike your own? What surprised you most about South Africa as shown in this book?
2. Sindi points out several things her American friends would say or do. What differences do you see between the South African worldview and the American worldview Sindi has been briefly exposed to?
3. Respect is very important in African culture. How would this story be different if the characters were from your community?
4. Sindi is afraid people will find out her father has HIV. How would you feel if you lived next door to someone with HIV? Would you respond any differently if the person had cancer?
5. Why do you think Sindi's parents aren't willing to talk about HIV even within the family?
6. In the Prologue Sindi says, "It hurts to fall, but you get up; you keep skating." In what ways is Sindi hurt by the things that are happening in her life? Why isn't continuing to go through the motions of normal life enough to solve those problems?
7. How is Solly hurt by his father's illness and death? In your culture, how do boys learn how to be men?
8. Why do you think Solly understands Sindi's love of skating better than other family members? How difficult do you think it was for him to sell his skates? Why do you think he did?

9. How does her skating define who Sindi is? How does NOT skating affect her image of herself? Why doesn't Sindi want her family to know when she watches skating on TV?
10. Why does Sindi buy her mother a cheap vase for Christmas?
11. In order to hide the family's secret, Sindi cuts herself off from friendships. How do you think the different characters would have reacted if they found out? Why?
12. In Chapter 21 Jabu ridicules Sindi's suggestion that she should be tested. Why do you think she reacts so strongly?
13. Why do you think Jabu gets involved with someone like Makatso?
14. Makatso jokes about HIV. In what ways do young adults you know take risks while denying that anything bad will happen to them?
15. Which characters model living positively with HIV? In what ways? Can you think of other difficulties where these ways of coping might be helpful?
16. What unwholesome ways do you see people in the story responding to HIV? What makes these responses unhealthy?
17. What is MakaLerato's advice to Jabu (pp. 163-4)? Do you agree or disagree? Why?
18. Friendship and community are significant themes in the book. In what ways do friends and community help you in difficult times?
19. Several churches are mentioned: Wonderful Words of Life in Tembisa; the Khumalo's mostly-white former church in Kempton Park; the small Baptist chapel on the ridge in KwaZulu; and Uncle Njabulo's Apostolic congregation by the river. How do they differ? Which would you most like to visit and why?
20. How is leprosy (Hanson's Disease) in biblical times similar to HIV today? How are they different? How do you think Jesus would treat someone with HIV if he lived in your community today? Why would that encourage someone living with HIV?

Other YA Books by LeAnne Hardy

All books are available from Amazon.com in print or e-book format. Signed copies may be obtained from the author at no extra charge. See www.leannehardy.net for the author's full range of titles.

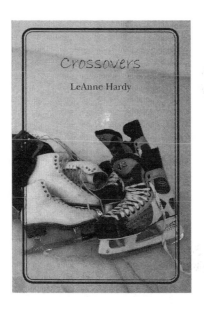

Crossovers (ages 10 to 13)
Birch Island Books

When Sindi's friend Ben was a thirteen-year-old hockey player wanting to learn to jump and spin, he was scared to death the guys would find out. He didn't even want to think about what his former-hockey-star father would say.

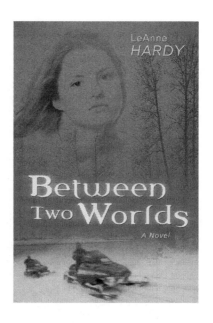

Between Two Worlds (ages 12 and up)
Kregel Publications, Grand Rapids, MI

Cristina Larson is American. Or is she? She grew up in Brazil and feels like a Brazilian. Jason Erickson is the one who is American. Or is he? His grandmother came from Korea. He doesn't look like his Swedish-American neighbors in Rum River, Minnesota. And sometimes being different can be downright dangerous.

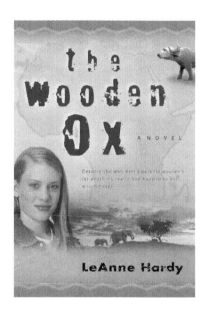

The Wooden Ox (ages 10 and up)
Kregel/Birch Island Books

Despite the war, Keri's parents wouldn't let anything really bad happen to her … would they? But when rebels attack the village where the Andersons are distributing clothes to the needy, there is little her parents can do to protect Keri and her brother. Does God care enough to help them? And what about the African boy soldier they befriend?

Made in the USA
Middletown, DE
11 September 2018